Verity

To Doreen
In Friendship

Marian Engel

First Published in Canada 2014 by Influence Publishing

Story Development Editor: Jodie Dias
Development Editor: Nancy Wickham
Cover Art Concept: Wendy Watson
Book Cover Design: Marla Thompson
Typeset: Greg Salisbury
Photographer: Wendy Watson

Verity

Marian Keen

This book is dedicated to the memory of
Penelope Gray-Allan
who typed the first draft and encouraged me
to publish the story of Verity.

The past is a mirror.
In it we perceive
The insights we need
To find true harmony.

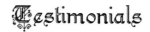Testimonials

"The story of Verity's growth ... is bewitching and engrossing, and the inclusion of magic and the depth of detail really took this tale beyond a simple fairy tale retelling to a full-blown medieval fantasy."
Judge, Writer's Digest 21st Annual Self-Published Book Awards

"Verity whisks the reader into a compelling medieval fantasy world, wrought with the same issues young people face in reality today. Despite adversity, the young heroine remains true to herself, a loyal friend, and a strong role model for readers."
Laura Pearson, Teacher Librarian, École Elémentaire William Bridge Elementary School

"Marian Keen has written a new kind of fairytale in which happy endings are all about following your heart. It's an imaginative tale brimming with all the magic you could hope for, and at the same time is bold in its honesty about the challenges that confront young people. The character of Verity learns to embrace her truth—this becomes her secret power."
Brock Tully, Founder of the World Kindness Concert, Author of "The Great Gift for Someone Special"

"Verity takes the reader on a fascinating trip led by a brave young heroine. The main character is a role model the reader can truly connect with, and the book is as entertaining as it is inspiring. The message about the importance of staying true to yourself and rising above life's obstacles is highly relevant for youth in today's world."
Alyson Jones, President of Alyson Jones and Associates, Child and Family Therapist, Author of "MORE: A New Philosophy for Exceptional Living"

Acknowledgements

A book is a compilation of the efforts of many people. It is not possible to acknowledge them all on one page, so I must adhere to those who have given me the essential support for this book.

I would like to express my thanks to:

Julie Salisbury, my publisher, for her enthusiasm and belief in the value of my insights, and her team at Influence Publishing, especially in-house editor Nina Shoroplova for her attention to detail and clarity, and project manager Gulnar Patel who keeps us all on track.

Nancy Wickham, my right hand editor, for her infinite patience and meticulous talent.

The men in my family: Bill, my life partner and husband, whose support never fails; Gary, my son, who applauds me in all my creativity; and John, my son-in-law, who gives inspiration to my writing. All three men show their support by cooking amazing meals and relieving me of that responsibility so I can create stories.

The women in my family: my daughter Wendy, who has extensive technical know-how and is an amazing artist; and my daughter Jodie, who illustrates my children's stories with whimsy and historical truth and looks after me like a mother hen.

Thank you to Alyson Jones, Laura Pearson, and Brock Tully for reviewing my manuscript and kindly providing testimonials.

And finally, to Hannah Lemdersi, whose love of the story made me seek its publication.

Table of Contents

DEDICATION
TESTIMONIALS
ACKNOWLEDGEMENTS
CONTENTS
CHARACTERS
PROLOGUE

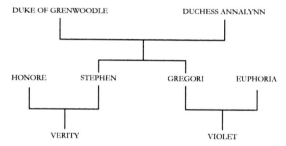

DUKE OF GRENWOODLE   DUCHESS ANNALYNN

HONORE   STEPHEN   GREGORI   EUPHORIA

VERITY   VIOLET

The Grenwoodles

Characters

Agatha, Scullery Maid
Annalynn, Duchess, Verity's Grandmother
Arthur de Cortelaide, Marquis, married to Isabella
Balford, Baron von, Nobleman owning adjacent property
Bennefield, Sir, a Knight
Cerric, Brother, First Tutor to Verity and Violet
Darcus, Euphoria's Henchman
Delancey, Brother, Second Tutor to Verity and Violet
Euphoria, Duchess, Violet's Mother
Fiametta, Lady's Maid to Isabella de Cortelaide
Frederick, Sir, Overseer at Greenwoodle Castle, Verity's "Father"
Garrod, Stable Boy
Granny Neddith, Older Woman who lives in Grenwoodle
Gregori, Duke, Violet's Father
Grenwoodle, Duke, Verity's Grandfather
Honore, Lady, Married to Stephen, Verity's Mother
Isabella de Cortelaide, Marquise, married to Arthur
Kailan, Governess to Verity and Violet
Lucien de Cortelaide, Son of Arthur and Isabella
Mortimer, Valet to Arthur de Cortelaide
Nicholas, Prince
Pagley, Lady's Maid to Isabella de Cortelaide
Prudence, Lady, Infant Verity's Nursemaid and "Mother"
Rothko, the Raven
Stephen, Lord, Verity's Father
Verity, Heroine
Violet, Daughter of Gregori and Euphoria
Walther, Valet to Prince Nicholas, King's Counsel
Wizard of the Wood, Wizard

Prologue

The rasps and clanks of a hundred swords swirled the morning mist as the battle between the knights of the green plume and the knights of the red plume grew fierce. Spurts of scarlet flew through the air and dripped down the long-stemmed grass. It was a dark day in the darkest of the Middle Ages when noblemen fought over the riches of the precious land.

A solitary raven watched as the knights of the red plume began to falter under the swords of the green-plumed knights. His beady eye fixed on their tiring leader whose sword slowed as he became disheartened. Another pair of eyes observed the leader's red plume as it moved ever closer to the edge of the meadow to escape from the horror of defeat. Those steady eyes and flashing sword progressed through the mayhem to the same destination but with a different purpose. Once in the woods, the two leaders faced each other in a leaf-lined clearing under the wise old oaks.

A third sword gleamed, half hidden by a gooseberry bush. Friend or foe? The raging battle between the two nobles was fierce but short, as one sword found its mark and the red plume and red blood graced the rooted ground.

Detecting a new sound behind him, the noble of the green plume held his panting breath and stepped quickly to his right, ready to turn his sword to more defence, but he was too late. A pain of fire pierced his side and he staggered to lean against the trunk of the mighty oak for support as he painfully raised his sword. His eyes focused on the tall figure of his younger son, who had struck him.

"Gregori!" he burst out in sharp surprise.

"Yes, Father. It is I!" said his son, through gritted teeth, balancing his sword in readiness to finish what he had begun.

"Why, my son?" whispered the bleeding nobleman.

"You said it yourself, Father. These fertile lands of Burgundy will provide our riches. They will gain us anything we want and I want them to gain the hand of Lady Euphoria of San Darconia.

She will not take promises for the future. She wants it now! And so do I!" He stepped forward and prepared to thrust the red edges of his sword again at the weakened figure of his own father.

From the meadow, a light-timbred voice called, "Father!" The elder man—The Duke of Grenwoodle—parried the murderous blade and extended his boot to step sharply on his son's foot.

"You must be drunk, Gregori!" he said.

The young man winced and stumbled to his knees just as the sound of other voices approached.

"I saw him come this way," called the same light voice.

The green-plumed nobleman stood tall over his son and said, "Here comes your brother. We will deal with this matter another day when you're sober. Arise and look the part of a faithful son, but do not return to the castle. It is no longer home to you. You love your sword and a greedy dame; so, seek your own fortune. Mine will not be yours. Go, now, and your mother will never know the truth from me."

The knights crashed through the berry brush with gasps of dismay when they saw their wounded leader, the Duke of Grenwoodle. A fair-haired youth with light step was the first to reach and support the wounded nobleman.

"Are you all right, Father?" he asked.

"Only a scratch, Stephen," replied his father. "Is the battle done?"

"We won!" chorused the knights. "For our land! For our Duke! For our women! For our God!"

The Duke smiled at their enthusiasm, though he felt no joy in victory that day. He leaned gratefully on the light frame of his elder son and, without a backward glance, followed the exuberant knights out of the woods and into the clearing where the gory remains of their victory seeped into the ground.

No one but the raven watched the brooding figure of the Duke's younger son Gregori retreat further into the forest until he was swallowed by the greenery.

The solitary black bird observed the activity for a while and then, satisfied that the Duke was preparing to return home, swooped out of the giant oak and circled up and up toward the swelling clouds. When at last he spied the lake, he flew straight on purpose to report all that he had witnessed.

* * * *

Within a year of the battle in the forest glade, the Duke's elder son Stephen married Lady Honore. She was as fair-haired as her husband and was loved for her kindness to all, including animals. Soon a baby daughter arrived with sunny smiles for everyone and eyes of the deepest and truest blue.

For a time, joy reigned in the castle. But then a pestilence known as the Black Plague took one by one—Honore, then Stephen, then the Duke, and finally his wife Annalynn. The baby girl, Verity, was spared.

The Overseer, Sir Frederick, best friend of Stephen, was highly respected by the knights and peasants alike, as he did his best to maintain the Grenwoodle estate in the aftermath of the bubonic plague.

A cousin of Lady Honore's, Lady Prudence, looked after Verity as if the child were her own.

Then one day, word arrived that the younger son of the Duke was returning to claim his inheritance.

Chapter 1

SUNSHINE THREATENED

The honey curls of the laughing toddler bounced as she ran in the garden. Prudence, her governess, cautioned her to beware of the rose thorns and then turned to the assistant cook who had just described her latest accomplishment with spun honey.

"You have learned it just in time to impress the new Duke. He will be here in a fortnight to claim his inheritance and she," the governess nodded toward the baby girl and continued bitterly, "will be banished to a nunnery."

"Perhaps not," said the cook. "Perhaps he'll have a generous heart. She is family after all—his only niece. Perhaps he'll have family of his own for her to play with. Perhaps …"

"Oh, do be silent! We could 'perhaps' all day and never guess the future. Besides, at midday tomorrow we will find out. Sir Frederick has promised to prepare us for the new Duke. I just hope he's healthy! I've had enough of people dying."

"I know," whispered the cook. "The Black Death! It took so many in my old village. We who survived had to leave, but when I came here, the Duke's son and his young wife were among the first to die. I hope it's over."

"Indeed. I hope it's over, too. I was here when the dying started."

"The plague!" muttered the cook, gathering herbs.

"No! The battle in the meadow. We could hear the shrieks and the clanging of the swords from the tower. Milady Annalynn was so afraid. She wept. She wrung her hands. Her whole family was in the meadow. And then…"

"What?" asked the cook.

1

"Her raven returned and she bade me leave, but as I went down the stairs, I heard her cry out."

"What happened? Did the raven attack her?"

"No. Not at all. But Milady left the tower and buried her younger son's possessions before the knights returned. And, of course, he did not return."

"How did she know?"

"I am sure that somehow the raven told her."

"The bird? How did he carry such a message?"

"I don't know. I saw nothing before she bade me leave, but she knew her son would not be back, and she buried his things in that rose garden."

"Hmm," pondered the cook, looking at the red roses.

"Things got better for a while when Master Stephen married, and his little 'Sunshine'—Verity with her golden curls—was born."

"Too bad the Duke didn't live long enough to enjoy his granddaughter."

"Life can be so cruel," said Prudence. "Parents and grandparents, taken by the Black Death, left that sweet little child all alone in the world."

The cook sighed, and then brightened, "But now we know that the younger son didn't die. He's coming back to claim his title. He'll look after his little niece—you'll see!"

She shook her bag of gathered rose petals. "Now I'd best return to the kitchen. See you tomorrow in the Great Hall!" The cook bustled off.

"Yes," murmured Prudence, her eyes steadily watching the toddler. *No wonder your father always called you 'Sunshine,'* she thought fondly and then said aloud, "I vow I'll never let any harm come to you. I'll..."

She broke off as she heard voices coming from behind the hedge. First, she recognized the voice of Sir Frederick. She listened then with more attention. Finally she realized that the low rumbling sound was that of the Wizard of the Wood.

Sir Frederick's voice sounded frantic. "She is in grave danger I'm telling you. The word is he practices black magic. He's ruthless! People who have crossed him have died mysteriously. What chance has an innocent toddler against his evil?"

The governess gasped, glanced at the baby girl, and moved closer to the hedge. She listened attentively to the low rumble of the Wizard's voice.

"Does he know about the baby's birth?"

"He could. I can't be certain."

"I see," continued the Wizard. "Then the Black Death must have another victim."

"What?" exclaimed the knight. "I want to protect her, not kill her!"

The governess covered her mouth to stifle a gasp.

"Now do not panic, Sir Frederick. Just prepare for a little risk. Can you do that?"

"Yes. Yes, anything!"

"Good! You have arranged the meeting in the Great Hall for midday tomorrow as I instructed?" There was a mumbled "Yes" in reply. "Then tonight you must get married. Can you do that?"

"Who?" croaked Sir Frederick.

"Doesn't matter—anyone you like—perhaps the governess, Lady Prudence?" asked the Wizard. "Is she fond of the little girl?"

"Yes… yes… perhaps. I'll try…"

"Good! Tonight you get married and tomorrow, in the Great Hall, the Black Death will claim another."

Prudence, faint with alarm, turned quickly, scooped up the toddler, and entered the castle by the scullery.

"There is no way this side of heaven or hell you will be in the Great Hall tomorrow, my little Sunshine. I will see to that!" vowed the governess.

Baby Verity giggled and cooed at being jostled as the governess hurried to hide her away in the nursery. Prudence slowed her steps as another thought mellowed her panic. *Married?* Would she consider marrying Sir Frederick? The thought was not without merit. She slowed even more as she contemplated the idea. Blonde curls shook as the toddler invited more jiggling. Absentmindedly, Prudence bounced the wee one up and down as she thought of Sir Frederick's deep brown eyes—so like her own. His broad shoulders were so...

"What am I thinking?" she scolded herself aloud. "He's planning to..."

What exactly? She did not know. She had only heard some of the conversation, but it involved the Black Death in the Great Hall tomorrow at midday.

Perhaps if I married him tonight, I could find out his plan, she thought with a cunning smile as she entered the sanctuary of the nursery.

Chapter 2

A WEDDING

Later that night by the candle's dim light, the governess watched a small frown cloud the sleeping face of her innocent ward. *Perhaps she anticipates tomorrow's treachery,* thought the governess. "Don't worry little one, I shall protect you. I promise." The frown melted into serenity as if the sleeping child understood Prudence's thoughts.

The governess smoothed a wrinkle from her favourite dress and tucked in a stray wisp of her chestnut hair. She glanced at the candle and frowned.

"It's late. He's chosen not to marry me. Of course, I've passed my twentieth birthday. He's probably chosen to marry that buxom scullery girl who flirts with all the knights. She'll do anything… I'm just a third-rate distant cousin, and poor at that. I'm lucky to have a roof over my head and a decent charge… such a dear one."

She adjusted the child's night cover. "If worse comes to worst, I could run away with the wee babe!"

A muffled rap on the door was so faint she did not hear it for the intensity of her thoughts. Rap, rap! It sounded louder. Her heart pounded and she thought the sound might be coming from her own chest. Holding the candle with a shaking hand, she quietly opened the door. The scullery maid's flushed face greeted her.

Her first thought, *He did marry the little…* was interrupted.

"Milady, the Overseer, Sir Frederick, bade me fetch ye now. He said as long as the babe is asleep, I should watch her for ye. Milady, he's in the Great Hall an' says ye should go there now. Please, Milady."

The governess swallowed. Her throat was dry. The maid looked perplexed at her silence. "Is the babe asleep then, Milady?"

"Yes," Prudence croaked, then cleared her throat. "Yes, she's asleep. I won't be long." As the maid padded quietly over to the cradle, Prudence slipped out the door.

Flying down the stairs, heart pounding, the governess carefully held her skirts. "No good to trip now and muckle myself when I'm about to find out the truth, for little Verity. That's odd— Verity means truth."

Holding that thought, she entered the Great Hall. In the dim light coming from the far doorway of the Chapel, she could see Sir Frederick speaking to a tall figure in a black robe. A hood covered the man's face and she thought of the Black Death and shivered before common sense told her it must be the priest.

Seeing Lady Prudence, Sir Frederick strode across the Hall and took her hand gently in his.

"I've long admired you from afar... I... I've thought of you often," he began, and then stumbled, "I've... I... ah... uh... This is difficult. You needn't be frightened," he blurted as he saw the look in Prudence's eyes as she gazed at the hooded priest.

"Then tell me the truth," she pleaded.

"Yes. The truth! The truth is I want to protect 'Sunshine' from evil. Stephen was my best friend and I owe him that. You are an honest woman. In fact, you are the only woman I trust, so I must ask you bluntly. I fear it may anger you, but I must. Would you trust me? Would you help me? Would you marry me, so that we can protect the child together?"

"Of course," she said quietly.

He looked at her face. Seconds ticked by slowly. He saw her trust in the steady gaze she returned. He lifted her hand and bent his head to gently kiss her palm. Then the two followed the priest into the Chapel.

The priest removed his hood and the ceremony began by the candlelit altar.

With beating heart, the governess vowed, "I, Prudence, take thee..."

"Frederick," said the priest.

"Frederick," repeated Prudence, "to be my husband…"

Chapter 3

THE TOWER

How to keep a baby amused, thought Prudence: *just move her in the middle of the night!* Verity was toddling around, exploring her new quarters with delight. As Prudence kept an eye on the child, she tidied the room and reflected on the past night with amazement. "Sir Frederick—Frederick—is my husband."

She remembered his urgent orders as she, the scullery maid, and the priest moved all her possessions and those of the baby to Frederick's spacious quarters on the other side of the castle. This morning, Prudence had awakened to sunshine lighting the room. Now she would be living on the south side of the castle. The view of the lake had been pleasant, but it was on the north side and had always seemed cold.

Wondering what her new view would show from the window, she approached and opened the shutter wide. Green fields stretched across her view. Up with the sun, the field hands and gardeners were already hard at work. Her chest swelled with pleasure at the sight. She appreciated the honest labourers and the sweet smell of the newly mown hay. This view was much more alive and uplifting than the bleak prospect of the cold lake. She shivered as she recalled that these same peasants would be gathering in the Great Hall at midday today. For what purpose? She still did not know.

Frederick had pleaded, "Trust me!" and she did, but she couldn't be sure that she trusted the mysterious Wizard of the Woods. None of her questions could be answered last night because they were too occupied with the task of stealing the child and moving all their goods.

What had Frederick said? "Keep her out of sight today and find something to cover her hair of sunlight before Duke Gregori arrives. One look at her and he'd guess she is his brother's child."

"What good will that do?" she'd asked him. "People will tell him anyway."

"Not if the Wizard's plan works. Let us wait and see what happens in the Hall tomorrow."

And now it was tomorrow and she had already worked out a solution to the child's golden locks. She used the boiled root that her own mother had used to darken her hair when it had silvered. The child had struggled and protested vigorously when Prudence had washed her hair. But once it was dried and brushed, the child was unaware that now she had brown hair just a shade lighter than Prudence's own.

Now Prudence began to see the Wizard's plan. She understood that the younger brother, now to be the new Duke, had a wicked reputation. He was known to be greedy and would tolerate no one in his way. If he were to suspect that Verity had a claim, even a minor one, to the estate of his father, he could remove her to a nunnery. However, if the new Duke does not know he has a niece, and believes her to be the child of his Overseer, Sir Frederick, and herself, then Verity could have a safe and pleasant life. If the Duke found out he'd been deceived, they could all forfeit their lives. But how did the Wizard expect to keep the castle and village populace from telling the Duke?

Prudence's hand flew to her mouth. Of course! The Black Death! He would threaten them with the plague! We must get far away from the Hall. Verity cannot be subjected to such a risk!

Prudence started in alarm at the sound of the horn calling everyone to the Great Hall. Still at the window, she watched as the peasants dropped their tools and headed for the castle. Prudence spun around.

She thought, *I must hide her now, but where? Ah! The Tower! No one dares to venture there because of the raven.*

"Come, Verity," Prudence urged. "Quickly, Poppet! The raven will not harm you; he will be your protection."

Prudence seized the child and left the room. She ran through the dingy corridors, ducking into rooms and side passages to avoid the people on their way to the Great Hall.

Finally, she heard no approaching footsteps and hastened around a corner—*ooof!*—into the arms of the priest!

"There, my child, you are going the wrong way!"

"No!" blurted Prudence, "I mean yes, I know. I've just been sent to fetch a wimple. I won't be long."

"Very well," answered the priest, "I'll carry the child so you can do your errand quickly."

"N-no!" Prudence protested, but the baby grabbed his rosary and began to inspect it as she slid into his arms. Prudence's heart sank.

Just as the priest stepped away, a feeble voice called, "Father!"

Granny Neddith scuffed slowly along the passage, leaning on her cane. "Where am I supposed to go?" she wheezed.

The priest silently handed the baby back to her governess. "Don't be long," he said in a low voice and, taking Granny's free arm, he steadied her as they walked down the passageway.

With a sigh of relief, Prudence hurried on, her arms wrapped tightly around the child. She entered the Chamber of the former Duchess Annalynn. She hesitated by the wall sconce as her fingers felt out a familiar crevice in the wall. She touched a hidden lever and a portion of the wall moved away. Slipping through, Prudence closed the opening and ascended the stairs that were faintly lit by the daylight from above.

Verity was delighted to explore the Tower room. She pushed her tiny fingers into every crevice she could find so that she, too, could make the wall move. Very patiently for such a young child, Verity methodically worked her way around the curve of the wall. Prudence smiled at the child's futile efforts. She rested her head against the back of the chair that Verity's grandmother Annalynn had kept with her writing table in the tower.

What did she feel compelled to write? Prudence wondered. *So few people can read and even fewer can write. Just the same, I wish I could read,* she thought and closed her eyes and dozed. She dreamed of the

Wizard. He was chasing her through the woods. Her legs were so tired that she was running very slowly. The Wizard called, "Stop, woman. I will put a spell on you!"

"No!" she cried, "I do not wish to suffer the Black Death!"

"Do not be foolish, woman. My spell will make you read." He touched her with his wand and it made a snapping sound. Terrified, she brushed the wand away. The Wizard started to melt, but the wand scraped against her arm with a grating sound. A childish giggle drifted up from a hole at her feet, and something hard and heavy slammed onto her knees. She awoke with a start.

Verity was pushing an ebony writing box onto Prudence's lap. She reached to steady it and looked past the child at an opening low in the wall.

She sat up with a start. This wasn't a dream. Verity had found her grandmother's hiding place.

Prudence opened the box slowly. Nestled at the front were two white goose feathers with ink-stained tips. The ink in the well had dried up long ago.

Verity's pudgy fingers reached for a feather. She brushed its softness against her cheek in sheer delight and turned away with her treasure. The rest of the contents were rolls of parchment filled with delicate traces of ink. Prudence knew they formed words, but stared at them helplessly.

A shadow fell across the parchment. Prudence twisted to see the raven on the window ledge eyeing her suspiciously. She snapped the box closed and hastily returned it to its hiding place. She pushed back the covering stone. Fearfully, she turned to the fluttering behind her. To her astonishment, the raven waddled over to Verity who reached out unafraid and patted the glistening black feathers of the bird. The raven tasted the child's brown hair with his tongue. He turned his black eyes back to Prudence, who was holding her breath in alarm.

"Nice birdie," she faltered. In that moment, she almost imagined the bird smiling at her, but then a tremendous moan rose from below, and she moved quickly to the window to see what was happening. She thought the sound came from the Great Hall, and she was glad she had not gone, but feared the result just the same.

A strange voice behind her said, "Stay true to your secret; all will be well."

She spun around in alarm only to see the raven take flight and rise out through the window.

Verity ran after him, "Birdie!" She was too small to see, as only Prudence could, the black wings glide swiftly toward the Wizard's Wood.

Movement below drew her attention. People were leaving the Great Hall. Prudence picked up Verity, who was still playing with the feather, and rushed down the stairs. At last, Prudence turned a corner near the Great Hall and slipped into a circle of gossipers.

"So exciting! Our Duke will soon return and bring his wife and child. Grenwoodle will be happy once again," said one.

"Too bad we have such sad news for him: his mother and father, brother and his wife and their child, all dead of the plague!"

"So sad, indeed. Especially that child! She had such a sunny disposition. But we mustn't dwell on past losses. We have a welcome to prepare. The Duke is expected within a fortnight. We have no time to spare. Let us go and make our plans."

One woman stopped and patted Verity's soft little arm. "Your little Verity is so sweet, Prudence. It was God's will that the plague would leave your family whole. We are grateful for that at least!" She hurried off after the others, leaving Prudence wide-eyed with shock and surprise.

"There you are, my dear!" said Frederick. "I did not see you in the Great Hall."

"I was late, so I stayed at the back," ventured Prudence.

"Wasn't the Wizard wonderful, my dear?"

"Yes! Of course! The Wizard!"

"Such a great plan! Asking us to cooperate so he could put a spell on us to protect us against the Black Plague. Of course we had to agree. Now, we have absolutely nothing to fear. We were all so sad, remembering how we lost the Duke's granddaughter. She was such a ray of sunshine! But we mustn't dwell on past losses now. You and I are so fortunate that it was God's will to leave our family whole. Dear Verity, your mother and I are so happy you are well, aren't we, my dear?"

"Y-y-yes! Of course!" answered Prudence, stunned. Now, at last, she knew the truth. The Wizard had put a spell on everyone to believe that Sunshine, Stephen's daughter, had died but that "their daughter" Verity had survived. She would have to keep her knowledge secret. She remembered the strange voice in the tower that said, "Stay true to your secret; all will be well."

Prudence shivered. Then, she smiled. Such an easy secret to keep. Verity was hers! She continued on with her husband, smiling and exchanging pleasantries as they walked. Clutching her white feather, Verity put her head on her new mother's shoulder and fell asleep.

Chapter 4

SUBTERFUGE

The following days were full of joyous preparations for the arrival of the Duke and his family. Their private quarters were cleaned and aired. The kitchen hummed as all the specialties of the house were readied. The field labourers sang as they worked gathering in the crops that were ripe and weeding around those still growing. The stables were cleaned out and the animals groomed for inspection. The carpenters toiled at repairs and improvements, but still found time to build a special carved bed for the Duke's daughter. The castle knights chose a cream-coloured steed of royal bearing as a gift for the new Duke; the best seamstress created a heavenly velvet dress for the new Duchess in a glowing blue colour called "azure." Goldsmiths prepared new rings with the seal of the Duchy and the personal names of the Duke and Duchess: Gregori and Euphoria.

Prudence had never enjoyed life more. She ordered linens for the Duchess's chamber and made an intricate lace dress insert as a personal gift for the Duchess. But her greatest pleasure came from spending hours in the garden with Verity. The child was beginning to talk fluently now and called her "Mama" as the new nursery-maid was teaching her to do.

Frederick was most attentive and Prudence enjoyed his authoritative command as he temporarily ruled the castle.

One day in the garden, his eyes followed her as if mesmerized by her every move.

"Why are you staring at me?" she asked with a slight unease.

He answered in wonder, "It seems as though we are newly-weds, my dear. I find it hard to believe we've been married for three years! It seems like only last month we took our vows. I do love you so!"

Prudence choked on the berry she had just swallowed. Frederick quickly thumped her on the back and laughed.

"Just because I express a sentiment, you needn't choke."

Prudence caught her breath and composed her thoughts. "Just a seed, my love. I'm fine and I agree. Marriage feels new to me also."

Frederick grasped her hand and kissed it. "We'll just have to remind ourselves of the years by planning Verity's third birthday in two months."

"But she was born…" started Prudence and hesitated. She wondered whether the Wizard's spell had bewitched Frederick too. How could she rely on Frederick when she couldn't know what he actually believed?

Frederick put a hand on her shoulder, "You always get mixed up. Remember she arrived early. Never mind, she's healthy and so are you. That's all that matters. Enough! It's time for our little girl to have a ride on Daddy's shoulders. Come, Verity, let's have a gallop. Daddy will be the horse!"

Prudence sank gratefully onto a small garden bench. What a masterful spell the old Wizard had spun. She felt weak with relief at her own good fortune, but she knew she must take care to encourage the charade and let her husband lead the way. How very lucky she was! She wondered if her luck would hold when the new Duke arrived. As an exclamation to her thoughts, the castle horns began to trumpet—the first signal of the coming of the new master.

$\mathscr{C}$hapter 5

ARRIVAL AND ACCIDENT

Prudence dwelled in worry as she combed Verity's hair with more vigour than the toddler's fine hair needed. Verity began to whimper and raised her hands to stop the comb.

"Sorry, Sunshine..." Prudence bit her lip. "Mustn't make that mistake again!" she reprimanded herself. She straightened their clothes just as Kailan, the new nursemaid, knocked on the door.

Prudence opened the door with relief. She had confidence in Kailan and felt the girl would stand by her in trouble. Kailan had promised to let her know when the Duke's party was approaching the castle, so Prudence wouldn't have to wait in the hot sun amid the crowd with her young child.

Frederick had arranged for Kailan to journey from Prudence's own village to help the Duke's family. Kailan was marvellous with Verity, and Prudence had no doubt the Duchess would be pleased with her child-minding talents.

Kailan dipped a respectful curtsy. "They're not more than a few minutes away, Milady, and there's just enough time to reach the main stairs. The crowd is excited and careless. Best to stay back a bit, I'd say."

"Thank you, Kailan, I shall." They hurried down the passageway together, Kailan carrying Verity.

The cheers in the crowded courtyard echoed as the women approached the main entrance and stepped out into the bright sunlight. Prudence shaded her eyes and Kailan protected Verity's ears as the trumpets announced the arrival of the Duke's entourage.

Drumming hooves sounded on the drawbridge. Leading the guards on horseback was a slight and awkward youth on a big dark-grey horse. He charged into the Bailey as though he were trying to assault the castle. Following him, the guards trotted their horses in a controlled semi-circle and faced the entrance expectantly.

The youth fought to control his horse. He attempted to back his animal into the middle of the guards' circle.

At that moment, the villagers pressed forward, straining to see past the guards. One little boy pulled away from his mother's grasp and eagerly jumped forward to see better.

Neighing in protest, the grey horse backed up suddenly and violently through the guards' ring and into the crowd. The youth held on fiercely. Horse and boy could not avoid a shocking collision. The little boy shrieked as his leg snapped. The frightened horse then bucked, fatally striking the boy's mother desperately trying to reach her son. The confused youth astride the grey snapped his whip again and again. It was difficult to tell his intention, whether to keep the crowd back or force his mount forward.

Prudence heard the shrieking but she could not see over the crush of people at the top of the steps. Her apprehension rose. She feared the welcome was turning into a disaster. Some of the women turned away from the bloody sight below, giving Prudence a clear view of the lifeless body of a woman.

"Remove the injured boy and his mother!" ordered Frederick. "Take them to the Scullery!"

The stable hands gently lifted the young boy and carried him away from the chaos.

The crowd bristled with questions.

"What happened? Who's hurt?"

"It's young Garrod and his mother!"

"I think she's dead."

"They were kicked by that wicked grey horse."

A moment later the Duke and his wife passed under the portcullis on gleaming black horses.

The grey horse stepped forward and the youth pulled off his liripipe, revealing unruly black hair.

"I was first; I led the way," he shouted, struggling to control his mount.

"So you did, Darcus," answered the Duke, annoyed and dismissive. Turning to his wife he added dryly, "Your ward obviously could use more riding lessons."

As Prudence watched, the Duchess scanned the crowd with cold grey eyes, and a sneer emerged on her haughty face. She turned to the Duke and smiled triumphantly. "It appears Darcus has made an impression on the crowd."

Prudence then focused on the Duke. She saw the malicious curve of his mouth as he drew his wife's attention to the blood spattered on the stones. She could hear him say, "We draw first blood, my dear."

Prudence shivered.

In the years that followed, Prudence was frequently reminded of that first sight of the Duke and Duchess in the courtyard. She lived every day with a knot of fear that lay just under her heart. Prudence's knowledge of Verity's identity was a secret that could be dangerous for everyone, but most of all for Verity herself.

Chapter 6

THE HOUSEKEEPER

Shortly after arriving, the Duchess summoned Prudence and Verity to the nursery. Playing with a shiny bauble, the Duchess's daughter Violet seemed content. As the two children eyed each other shyly, the Duchess said to Prudence, "I understand you looked after the former Duke's granddaughter."

"Yes, Milady, I did," said Prudence as she curtsied.

The Duchess raised her chin a trifle and said, "Was it not difficult for you? You were with child yourself."

Prudence blushed in confusion and stammered, "I only looked after the baby a short time, Milady."

"I see," said the Duchess, watching her fixedly. "If it had lived, the child would have been nearly four. Is that right?" Prudence nodded meekly. "And Verity is how old?" the Duchess asked quickly.

"Her third birthday is coming up," answered Prudence, grateful that Frederick had unwittingly prepared her for this questioning.

"We must have a celebration then, my dear. Violet loves parties. She just turned four before we arrived," smiled the Duchess, gazing speculatively at the children. "Verity is such a tiny creature compared to Violet, but I wondered, because I noticed that Verity's speech is so well developed."

"Perhaps because I chatter too much!" Prudence responded impulsively.

"I hadn't noticed," the Duchess replied dryly. During the awkward pause, Prudence blushed. The Duchess continued, "I propose that Violet and Verity take lessons together."

"Lessons?" blurted Prudence in surprise.

"Yes, lessons. I wish Violet to learn the arts appropriate to womanhood, but I also insist that she learn to read and write. If two children study together, they may be more likely to apply themselves and take their studies more seriously. It will also be easier to acquire a teacher from the monastery. I will oversee their social skills and later teach them the herbal arts."

"I'm sure Verity will be honoured to be included in such an education," answered Prudence with mixed feelings. She prized the opportunity to read and write above all, but she feared the influence of the Duchess. She would have to watch carefully.

"One more request, Prudence!"

"Yes, Milady."

The Duchess continued to gaze at the children as if Prudence were not there.

"It is clear that Kailan is capable of watching both girls and they will be quite occupied. Thus, as you are free..." the Duchess's grey eyes stared into Prudence's brown eyes as she paused to emphasize her words. "I request that you oversee the kitchen, the general housekeeping of the castle, and the organization of its staff. Such duties are tiresome for me and I have more interesting occupations in mind. You don't mind, do you, my dear?" she asked as her gaze curled from the children and focused sideways at Prudence.

"N-n-n-no!" faltered Prudence.

"Fine! You may begin your duties today. Kailan and I will see to the children. Report only to me and do introduce the cook to the herb garden; his food is flat! That will be all, Prudence. You may go."

"Yes, Milady," Prudence bowed and found herself out in the hall alone and feeling empty. She wasn't sure how it had happened, but she was certain she had just lost her precious Verity and there was nothing she could do about it.

Chapter 7

SCRATCHED OUT

The months passed until one morning Prudence emerged from the Scullery door as Verity and Violet played ball with Kailan in the rose garden. Prudence felt a pleasant warmth as she watched her daughter laugh and play. Amid sudden squeals of delight, the ball spun in the air and landed in the middle of the roses. Both children rushed for possession. Bracing her feet, Violet abruptly pushed Verity's tiny body into the rose bush. Verity screamed. A running Kailan blocked Prudence's view as she also ran to help. A red smear like a rose petal spread on Verity's forehead. Her nose was scratched and her hands dirty. In seconds, Kailan had the child on the bench and was mopping up the blood when a cold voice stopped Prudence in mid-stride.

"Prudence!" called the Duchess, "I'm sure you have more important duties. Kailan is quite able to deal with a minor accident."

"B-b-but my child is hurt!" protested Prudence. She felt her face flush and her hands tremble. Never had she felt such anger, but where had the Duchess come from? She had been watching for some minutes with a broad view of the garden and yet she hadn't seen the Duchess until she spoke.

"I say it is nothing! Go check the number of bay leaves in today's stew. Cook is heavy handed. Go! That is an order!" said the Duchess.

Prudence hesitated, frustrated and confused at being treated like a servant. Her noble lineage was insulted. Her motherhood was thwarted. Kailan turned and nodded to her. Verity was all right. Prudence reluctantly retraced her steps to the door. She listened as Verity's sobs quickly subsided, and berated herself for being too protective; she had just reached the doorway when she heard the Duchess's imperious voice.

"Now, Verity, apologize to Violet for getting in her way."
"I'm sorry, Violet," said a small voice.
The knot in Prudence's chest twinged with pain.

Chapter 8

TWIST OF CONTROL

By the time another year had passed, Prudence had a clear picture of the ruthless nature of the Duchess. Kailan trusted and confided in Prudence the many incidences that she had witnessed of the Duchess's manipulations. Fear and anger twisted like vines around Prudence's heart. Then one day before cock's crow, Kailan sought her out to beg for help.

"I need your support. I'm afraid of her—of what she might do!" she begged.

"All the more reason you must follow her rules. Do not arrange anything behind her back," warned Prudence. "I'm sure Frederick can supply two men to accompany you on an outing with the children, but do not do it without her complete blessing."

"How do I accomplish that?" asked Kailan doubtfully. "The Duchess never blesses any of my ideas. You must understand. I have to get away from her eagle eye. She spies on me constantly. It can't be good for the children. They don't even laugh as they once did."

"Leave it to me," answered Prudence, "I'll think of a way. Now go to the nursery. Don't leave the children alone!"

The two women separated, furtively darting in opposite directions down the shadowy hallways.

Later, as if by chance, Prudence happened upon the children playing in the garden. With cook in tow, she was giving instructions about growing the herbs when she suddenly stopped, as if she was seeing the children for the first time. She stared a moment then shook her head and moved slowly away. She stopped, looked back at them again, and gave a sigh as she moved to the bed of parsley. She left the cook studying the leaves, crushing, smelling, and gathering according to Prudence's instructions.

Prudence retraced her steps, paused, stared at Violet, and sighed again. Startled, but not surprised, she felt tapered hands with long scarlet nails pulling on her arm.

"What do you see? What disturbs you about Violet?"

Prudence dropped a curtsy to the Duchess. "Sorry, Milady, 'tis not my place to say," she hung her head.

The Duchess grew impatient. "Don't be coy, Prudence. It does not become you. Is Violet ill?"

"Oh no, Milady. I was just thinking that Violet is such an intelligent child and it seemed to me she appears to be bored."

"Bored?" exclaimed the Duchess. "She's just a child! What gave you such an idea?"

Prudence hid her crossed fingers in the folds of her dress. She had to be careful that there could be no hint that the Duchess's hovering control was the cause. "I noticed that Violet doesn't laugh as she once did."

"What do you suggest?" asked the perplexed Duchess.

"Something to occupy her mind as you do yours with the study of herbs."

"Yes..." murmured the Duchess, unaware of the subtle flattery. "But, of course, she is so young."

"Young enough to play and learn. Kailan knows a great deal about flowers; the hills are covered with wildflowers at this time of year. They could make daisy chains and cornflower coronets. They could have a lovely time and begin an interest in plants."

"Beyond the castle grounds? It's unsafe!"

"Only if they went alone. I'm sure Frederick could supply proper escort..."

The Duchess watched as Violet sat amid the garden roses and picked apart a white rose. The petals fell upon her lap until the stem was barren. Violet yawned and threw it away.

"It is settled then, Prudence. Make the arrangements," said the Duchess. "Violet must have every opportunity. And, Verity must accompany her."

"Yes, of course," said Prudence, "I'll see to it at once."

She turned away quickly before the Duchess could see her

smiling with satisfaction. Prudence knew that the Duke was expecting an important visitor on the morrow and the Duchess would be occupied entertaining a guest. Kailan would have the children to herself.

Chapter 9

COTTAGE IN THE WOODS

In the long run, Prudence found that even subtle flattery wore so thin that it became transparent to the Duchess. However, by subterfuge, Kailan contrived again and again to take the little girls exploring; such interests excluded the Duchess.

Because Kailan was a natural teacher and kept activities interesting to her charges, the little girls loved her. Prudence's help was essential to the plan since she knew when the Duke and Duchess were occupied or travelling.

By the time Violet was eight years old, both girls had palfreys of their own. Palfreys were well suited for young women riders because their gait was smoother than that of warhorses. Their palfreys thrived as the groom fed them well and kept them clean for unannounced visits from the girls bringing carrots to their pets. One day, Violet's palfrey, Dolphus, went lame. The groom was beaten for carelessness and Dolphus was given to Verity. Verity's palfrey was given to Violet.

Verity was thrilled, because she loved Dolphus's white flame and stockings. She gave him even more treats and gentle kindness; she dismounted and walked when the ground was rough or steep. To everyone's relief, both palfrey and groom recovered.

One day, after a morning exploring the woods with the children, Kailan approached Prudence outside the Great Hall. Always interested in her daughter's welfare, Prudence asked if they had found the mushrooms they had been looking for.

"We did," said Kailan. "But we found more than that. Have you ever walked in the woods, Milady?"

"Not recently, why?" asked Prudence.

"We were looking at moss and lichens. It was cool and quiet

in the woods—too quiet. I felt observed. I looked around but I didn't see anyone. Then I realized a bird—a raven—was watching us. He followed us everywhere. Then I saw a cottage..."

Prudence took a startled breath.

"...by the brook," Kailan continued, "and I heard someone within. I took the children away before they saw it, for who knows who lives there! And they are very curious. Do you know who lives there?"

"Yes," said Prudence. "I believe it is the Wizard's lair and it is best, no doubt, to stay clear of it. You went too far, Kailan. You should be more careful."

"Yes. I realize that. We returned soon after that glimpse, you may be sure, but one thing more I found strange."

"Yes?" prompted Prudence.

"When Violet discovered her namesake flower, she started picking them excitedly. I looked around for Verity and saw her, a bit apart, petting the raven! The bird's tongue touched her hair. I was so frightened of him I froze to the ground, but Verity was quite calm and even brought back a feather from that bird. And... what do you think?"

"What?" asked Prudence, apprehensively.

"By the time we returned, the feather had turned white! Tell me," demanded Kailan, "is the raven a magical creature? Does he belong to the Wizard?"

"Did the bird speak?" asked Prudence.

"No. Not a croak. It was silent."

"Ah, well! Do not distress yourself, Kailan. Verity has a way with animals and birds."

"But, the feather?"

"She probably saw a goose feather and liked it better. Don't give it another thought!"

Chapter 10

A NASTY BIRD?

Kailan's next adventure made Prudence wish she had been more forthright about the raven. Kailan might then have been more prepared. But she had not told Prudence that she was going to take the children to the Tower. Unaware of the secret entrance, Kailan had merely explored the staircase from the main hall. Up, up, they had climbed and entered the chamber at the top. Lady Annalynn's desk and chair were still there, but the raven sat upon the sill, discouraging a peek at the view. Verity had begun to feel along the wall when the raven flew down and demanded her attention like a love-starved pet.

Verity laughed and patted his feathers. One dropped and, as she picked it up, it turned to white. Violet rushed to snatch it away, but as soon as she touched it, the feather once again turned black. Violet pushed the bird away and he croaked a loud raspy cry. Violet cried out in fright and they all left the Tower in haste.

As they descended the stairs, the Duchess suddenly appeared, blocking their descent. She demanded an explanation for their haste. Violet sobbed a story about a nasty, pecking bird in the Tower. Under the Duchess's orders, the Tower was sealed off from the hallway. No one but Prudence knew there was a secret passage to the Tower from the Master Bedchamber.

One day, Kailan sought out Prudence's guidance regarding the Duchess once again. "I must take the children out and away from her evil eye."

"Evil?" questioned Prudence. "Why do you say evil?"

She felt that familiar knot of apprehension tighten into a fear that travelled up the back of her neck to settle into an ache of despair. The same questions clouded her thoughts: how could she continue to endure the control that the Duchess maintained over her innocent daughter? Was the woman really evil?

"Well," Kailan explained, "perhaps 'evil' is a strong word, but the Duchess manipulates situations to Violet's benefit—even when Violet doesn't want her to. And Verity always loses."

"Does Verity ever complain to you?" asked Prudence.

"Verity is so sweet," said Kailan. "She loves Violet and is happy that Violet has the best of everything. She is not capable of jealousy and so is unconcerned."

"And Violet? How does she feel?" asked Prudence.

"She is happy as long as Verity is happy," said Kailan. "They both accept everything the Duchess dictates and continue to be content. But it cannot end well. I must contrive for the children to be away from the Duchess as often as I can. Can you tell me when the Duchess will be away for a day? I would like to take the girls down to the meadow by Lake Grenwoodle. There are unusual flowers there, I'm told, tall with red cups and black centres. They sound unlike any flower I've ever seen. I hope we can find them."

"I will endeavour to find out a time and let you know so you may have your wish," promised Prudence.

Chapter 11

MAGIC POND AND THREATS

Unfortunately, Kailan got her wish.

One morning early in the harvest season, Kailan sought the Duchess to ask for some coins and permission to take the children to the market for some threads and needles. Kailan thought it was time the children learned some needlework. But when she approached the Duchess's quarters, she was met by a cloud of dust. A maid was sweeping vigorously and only answered Kailan on the third inquiry.

"The Duchess?" the maid echoed, looking blankly at Kailan as if she'd never heard of any Duchess. "Oh! The Black Crow ye mean. She's flown off in a temper. First, she croaked at this one. Then, she croaked at that one. Nobody says nothin'. That made 'er madder and she lost her temper and hit old Jacko who's got hisself a purple eye. Then she gave us all so much work to do—we'll be lucky to get it finished before she comes back for vespers."

"You mean she'll be gone all day?"

"That's jus' wot I jus' said, ain't it? I tol' ye. Now go and let me get me work done."

"But where did she go?"

"Don't know. Don't care. She's croaked off, I tell ye, till eventide. Now go away!" the maid finished crossly, as she gave another big sweep with her broom. Kailan darted off before the dust cloud could reach her.

"She's gone for the day! This is our chance to visit the meadow by the lake." Abandoning her market plans, Kailan hurried to collect the children, never thinking to confide her new plan to Prudence.

Long before the heat of the day, Kailan and her two charges

entered the cool of the woods. Violet and Verity skipped ahead, singing the nursery rhymes Kailan had taught them. Kailan kept to a slower pace trying to ignore the ache in her foot where a horse had stepped on her when she was a child. She trudged along steadily, carrying the sack of food and the basket that would tote home the hoped-for flowers. She smiled at the happy youngsters, knowing they were relieved that they didn't have to struggle over tedious needlework and elated that they were in the woods. Kailan allowed them to run ahead as she knew their legs would give out long before the critical fork in the path.

A curve in the path blocked the children from Kailan's view. She could not hear them either. The sudden quiet was unnerving, but Kailan was a practical girl and she knew the children would spring into sight as soon as she reached the turn in the path. The only sound was the whisper of old leaves on the path as she trudged on. The whisper grew louder and louder. She found herself listening for some meaning in it. She stepped up her pace. The whispering filled her ears and confused her mind with elusive syllables. Her heart began to pound. What were the words? Where were the girls? What were the words? Where were the girls? Her mouth was dry with fear. She stopped abruptly to listen. Then she heard it clearly.

"Beware!" the whisper said and then faded into silence.

With her eyes on the turn in the path, Kailan ran. She tripped on a root and cried out, but regained her balance and held up her skirts with one hand as she rounded the corner.

There, sitting on the sunlit root of an oak tree, the two little girls intently watched a bug. Casually, Violet looked up.

"We decided to wait for you. Verity says it takes longer for old people."

Kailan's mouth gaped at the children. She felt a deep blush rise up and heat her face. She took pride in having a level head and yet here she was, thinking the Duchess—a mother—was an evil person, and hearing whispers when no one was there. She looked at the bug that so intrigued the children and was soon lost in teaching them about ladybugs.

By the time the three reached the fork in the path, Kailan took the right branch without a thought of the Wizard's cottage that lay hidden down the path to the left. The forest was dense and they had been walking downhill for a long time. Kailan began to feel uneasy about the climb back up the hill. Then the forest abruptly cleared and a lovely little pond danced in the sunshine.

Violet and Verity bared their feet in a blink and sat on the smooth flat rocks at the edge of the pond, dangling their feet in the cool, sparkling water. While they kicked and splashed, Kailan set out the meal and then she, too, enjoyed a refreshing dip for her feet.

"I like this water. It tingles!" announced Violet.

"It feels so good!" agreed Verity. "Look! The black and blue spot on my toe is gone! I thought I would have that bruise for a week."

Kailan looked at her own toes. Her crooked big toe often ached at the end of a long strenuous day with the girls. She closed her eyes and looked again. Her toe was straight! She covered her mouth to stifle a gasp. She stared at her perfectly formed toes.

"What's the matter, Kailan?" asked Verity.

"My toe is straight," answered Kailan shakily.

"Yes. Your toes are all straight. Don't you like straight toes?"

"But it's always been crooked," Kailan insisted, still staring at her feet.

"You're always telling us walking is good for us!" confirmed Violet. "I guess walking is good for you, too." Unconcerned, Violet broke off a piece of bread and began her meal.

Verity patted Kailan's shoulder. "Have some food, dear Kailan. You'll feel better." She passed the cheese and bread with a smiling glance over Kailan's shoulder. Kailan bit into the bread with sudden hunger, but noticing the direction of Verity's glance, she turned and there, once again, was the raven staring back at her. Kailan didn't care; she looked down and marvelled at her toe and then looked up again at the bird. A peaceful feeling took over her mind and she couldn't think of a thing to worry about.

Soon after, they pulled on their hose and shoes, and once more followed the path to the meadow. The grass was thick and deep and full of buttercups. Violet loved to make coronets from buttercups and set to gathering bunches of the yellow blooms. Kailan looked around vaguely and then sat down to help Violet. She felt mildly disappointed, but couldn't remember why and didn't really think it mattered when she could wiggle her toes and feel no pain. She started weaving the long stems of the buttercups and her eyes grew sleepy in the warm sunshine. Verity wandered along the edge of the meadow toward the Lake of Grenwoodle.

Ahead, Verity saw an old woman bent over in what looked like a bed of roses, but as she walked closer, she saw the red flowers weren't roses at all. Sharply pointed purple leaves formed a circle around drooping red shaggy petals, from which dangled threads that ended in black pods. The dark stems were covered with black thorns and the leaves curled like hands. The black-clad figure of the woman seemed to be gathering the flowers and placing them in a basket.

Verity saw a flower patch to her left and decided to help the woman gather her flowers. She walked through the meadow grass and looked closely at the red petals that covered the centre of each flower. She lifted the flower's head and screamed as the leaves grabbed her arm and the petals flew apart to reveal a ghastly face in the centre. Verity pulled back and fell into the slimy green swamp. *Splash!* Muck sucked her body down. She screamed again and suddenly the Duchess was above her, looking like a thundering black cloud with anger flashing in her icy eyes.

"What are you doing here, you vile child? This is my source! How dare you touch it?"

Verity looked in horror at the Duchess, whose hair straggled down in grey and black strands, whose mouth looked as vicious as a rabid dog's, and whose hands were covered with bloody scratches.

Verity sank deeper into the mire. She gasped and started to cry.

The Duchess bent closer to her, and in a rasping whisper said slowly and clearly, "If you say one word about what you saw here today, I shall see to it that your mother dies a slow and painful death, and that you, my pretty baby, will grow into a toad! Do you understand? Not one word to anyone!"

"Yes, Milady!" choked Verity, faintly.

"I can't hear you. Do you promise?" raged the haggard face above her.

"Yes! I promise!" cried Verity.

The Duchess reached down with her bloody hands and pulled Verity out of the quicksand by her clothes. She held her up like a kitten and, taking a few steps, dropped her on dry ground.

"Now forget what you saw and leave this meadow. If you say one word to your mother, you'll never see her again."

Verity was on her feet and running as soon as she turned away, but she felt a push from the Duchess's basket as she ran. Kailan was calling from higher ground and Verity ran as if Satan was pushing her.

"Verity! What happened to you?" exclaimed Kailan when she saw Verity pale and covered with muck. "Are you all right? You're bleeding!"

Verity's mouth worked silently. She was too frightened to speak. Kailan lifted her as Violet picked up their basket and they walked back up the path to the pond. The forest now cast a shadow on the water and it looked cold and uninviting, but Kailan undressed Verity, washed her, and wrapped her in her own shawl. Violet put her arm around her friend and the two watched soberly as Kailan washed the muddy clothes.

Kailan asked gently, "Was it quicksand? In a swamp?" Verity nodded, frightened lest she tell too much. Kailan said, "We shall never come this way again."

Soon, the three walked up the path to the castle. Not one of them remarked on the straightened toe, the bruise that had faded, the quicksand, or the bleeding gash in Verity's hand that had healed without a scar by evening.

The next morning, the Duchess appeared at breakfast. Her black hair shone. Her eyes sparkled with a blue fire. Her mouth curved in good humour and her pale slender hands showed not a trace of hard use.

The Duke, looking jovial and with burning eyes, kissed his wife, saying, "You never looked lovelier, my dear!"

Verity watched the Duchess warily and stayed as far from her as possible. Her strategy did not escape the attention of her mother. Prudence knew that something had happened, but she honoured her daughter's guarded look and asked no questions. Gratified that Verity was on her guard, Prudence realized that now there were three who knew that the Duchess was evil. But could they survive it?

Chapter 12

WOUNDED HERO

With the swiftly changing seasons came changes to the castle by the Lake of Grenwoodle. The servants grew haggard and more careful day by day. None would ignore, let alone defy, the Duchess. She ruled the castle by her will alone. Every day, the Duchess grew more beautiful, but colder.

The children were growing quickly too. One day, as the leaves turned to russet and gold, the long-ago-promised monk arrived. He imposed harsh discipline on the children, who up until now had only known Kailan's gentle disposition.

Brother Cerric was a scholar who had been totally absorbed in alchemy. He was confident he could find the secret of turning lead into gold to produce untold wealth for the Church and even have enough for his own advancement. Then, without warning, he had been assigned to teach two children how to read. Two girls! He was chagrined, but he must obey the Cardinal. He decided not to waste any time and so he imposed a stringent discipline on the two innocents—one quite spoiled, he noted—so that he could accomplish the task quickly and return to the monastery and his experiments.

Kailan's duties were reduced. She became little more than a servant who waited on her young charges like a nursemaid. Oddly, Kailan acquiesced without complaint. She had caught the eye of Sir Bennefield and had other thoughts on her mind.

Prudence knew that Brother Cerric was quite strict with the children, but she was so grateful that Verity would learn to read that she said nothing. Then one day she had more pressing thoughts on her mind. Duke Gregori had quarrelled with the neighbouring duchy and then, during a brief squabble of a battle,

Frederick had been wounded. Prudence dressed his wound daily and tried to make him comfortable. One evening, she began to fear for his life because it seemed he was dwindling away before her eyes. Prudence faced her life as she sat there listening to his laboured breathing. She realized that she had come to rely on his council and protection, and his position with the Duke. As Frederick's fever rose, he gripped her hand, and she knew she couldn't live without him. What would become of Verity and herself? She knew she loved him and he loved her. Her fear then became desperate.

When at last he slept, she slipped out of the room, candle in hand, to find help. Perhaps Kailan would know what to do. Candles flickered in the passageways as the castle's inhabitants settled themselves for the night. *The evening meal must be done,* she thought, as she headed for the old nursery where Kailan would be putting the girls to bed.

Prudence passed the Duchess's bedchamber. Up ahead was the nursery and she hastened. Then she stopped and gasped. There by the door was a monster! Tall and wide, it swayed. By the candle's light, she could see the surface ripple and the monster uttered a low moan. Then, it split into two and Prudence felt the blush of foolishness. Kailan's wide eyes blinked at her from the arms of her lover, Sir Bennefield. Prudence steadied her nerves and wished all monsters could be lovers in disguise.

"Kailan!" Prudence blurted. "Help me! Frederick is dying. Do you know a potion, a medicinal herb, an elixir, a spell, anything?"

As Prudence waved the candle back and forth with her trembling hand, Sir Bennefield smoothly took it from her hand.

"He's burning up!" Her voice rose in desperation. "What about that flower you were looking for—the red flower by the lake? Did you find it? Has it magic powers? Kailan?"

Kailan put her arms around her friend and held her as she cried. Kailan's eyes sought and questioned Bennefield's. He looked up and down the passageway. Nearby, a door closed with a thud. His eyes narrowed as he watched for a moment. Then he nodded to Kailan and, taking Prudence's arm, led her down the passage back to Frederick.

Kailan watched them go and then turned back into the nursery. She did not see the tight-lipped Duchess leaning against the door of her room. She did not hear as the Duchess cursed an innocent child. Nor was she aware that the Duchess plotted revenge on Verity, whom she thought had broken her promise, and told her mother and Kailan about the magic red flowers by the lake.

Chapter 13

BANISHED

Bennefield seemed like a giant to the people of the village; the tallest among them was a mere five foot one. Bennefield stood six foot four; his height frightened everyone except Kailan and the Wizard. The Wizard had once chuckled at Bennefield and told him he was ahead of his time.

"Someday, in another time when people fly and talk to others miles away, men like you will be commonplace. Instead of cowering in your presence, they will watch you play games in arenas."

Though Bennefield was a gentle man, he was a serious one. He never used his size in anger, but did find it useful on the battlefield. Frederick was his friend. It was Bennefield who had brought Frederick home from the last skirmish and delivered him to Prudence to nurse back to health. He had never thought the wounds to be fatal and was distressed as he guided the tearful Prudence back to her rooms.

By candlelight, Bennefield viewed his friend's pale face; he felt his cold hands. He removed the dressings and checked the wounds, and then he turned to Prudence. Her dark eyes were wide with fright and she held her husband's hands as though she'd never let go.

Bennefield knelt and smiled as he looked into her eyes. "Do not be so frightened, little lady! Your man will live to fight again. I know what he would do for me. He'd carry me off to our friend in the wood, he would. And I'll do the same."

Looking at his big face with the bigger grin, Prudence couldn't help but smile as she tried to imagine Frederick carrying this giant even a few paces. Then she grasped that he intended to take Frederick to the Wizard. Dismay crossed her face, but Bennefield patted her gently on the shoulder.

"It's all right. He'll be fine. The Wiz'll fix him up proper, you'll see." He gently gathered Frederick and his blanket into his arms and quietly walked out the door.

Prudence remained on her stool by the bed and slumped over and cried. Faintly, she heard the creak of the portcullis as the kindly gatekeeper allowed Bennefield out of the gate. Prudence stopped crying, but the hollow feeling in her heart told her she would never see Frederick again.

The Duchess's eyes and ears were everywhere, and Darcus had grown into a loyal and useful spy. With calculating eyes in a mean-spirited face, Darcus watched from the castle wall as Bennefield walked with his burden across the meadow toward the wood.

Swiftly, the Duchess's spy reported to her. "Bennefield is taking Sir Frederick to the Wizard of the Wood, Milady."

"What does he think that feeble old man can do? Chant a spell? Ha! One down and two to go. We shall take care of Lady Prudence in the morning, Darcus. Be ready."

"Yes, Milady." Darcus slithered down the hall.

The Duchess smiled to herself. "Soon you will have no one to protect you, little Miss blue eyes. No father. No mother. No nursemaid. And I shall turn you into a toad! Ha, ha, ha, ha, ha!"

The next morning drizzled. A raw chill seeped into the castle as Prudence hastened down to the kitchen to check on provisions for the coming winter. She had been absent from her duties for several days while she nursed Frederick, and was grateful she'd received no complaint from the Duchess.

As she suspected, the kitchen servants had holidayed in her absence. There was much to be done and, as she worked, she made mistakes because she was worried about Frederick. The noon meal was poor and she watched the Duchess carefully, expecting an outburst directed at her, but the Duchess seemed to ignore her. When the meal was done, the Duke gave the orders of the day. Nothing was said about the quality of the meal. Prudence breathed a sigh of relief and resumed her duties.

It was late in the afternoon when Prudence was summoned to the Duchess in the Great Hall.

Here comes my reproof, she thought, *but she is kindly speaking to me in private, saving me from humiliation. She knows of Frederick's illness.* She braced herself for her reprimand as she entered the Great Hall, but the Duchess was smiling at the Duke and seemed to be in good spirits.

"Greetings, Milady. Greetings, Milord," said Prudence, according to the castle custom. She curtsied with her head bowed.

"Yes, Prudence," said the Duchess. "Lord Grenwoodle and I were just speaking of you. So trustworthy. So conscientious, too. Such an excellent meal at noon today, for example. There seems to be nothing you can't do!"

The Duchess smiled again at her husband. The Duke frowned slightly and then uncertainly returned her smile. The Duchess looked back at Prudence with ice-cold grey eyes and suddenly Prudence began to tremble.

"I have a brilliant idea, Lady Prudence. One task that I can entrust only to you!

"I shall do my best, Milady," said Prudence with a tremor.

"I'm sure you will," said the Duchess with exaggerated satisfaction.

"What is the task, Milady?"

"You have such fine taste for fashion, my dear, I would like you to go shopping for me..."

"Sh-shopping?" queried Prudence.

"Yes. Shopping," affirmed the Duchess and added, "in Florence."

Prudence gasped. She couldn't leave Frederick and Verity for that many months. What was the Duchess thinking? She began to shake her head. The Duchess ignored her and presented a piece of parchment and a small purse.

"Here is the list of lace and materials I wish you to buy."

"But, Milady, I cannot read," protested Prudence, unheard.

"Here is a purse for the purchases, plus a sufficient amount for your travelling expenses."

"How can I go? I do not know how to get there!" wailed Prudence in a panic.

"Then ask!" smiled the Duchess.

"I have no means of transport."

"Supplied," shot back the Duchess.

"It will take me time to pack for the journey," faltered Prudence.

"It is done. Cart and mule await you in the Bailey. You will leave now. I suggest you hurry before the rains get too heavy."

"I must say goodbye to Frederick and Verity."

"Verity's studies must not be interrupted. I shall tell her myself so she will not be distressed. I shall tell Frederick when he recovers his strength." She pushed Prudence to the door.

Desperate, Prudence protested again, "But it is so late in the day to begin a journey."

"It will not be earlier if you tarry. Go now and spare Verity the agony of anticipated goodbyes. I shall take care of your daughter, never fear," she said as she pushed Prudence out of the castle and into the Bailey.

"Darcus has your cloak. He will accompany you. Remember, Prudence, buy the best cloth and the best lace. I'm sure you know there is much better than this!" She waved a piece of handmade lace and threw it on the ground in disgust.

Prudence barely had time to recognize her own bit of handmade lace before Darcus shoved her up and into the cart and led the mule through the gate and over the drawbridge. The cold drizzle dampened Prudence's skirts as she sat in the cart tightly clutching the purse and parchment. Her hands ached with the cold and her hair dripped before reality broke through the stunned shock and confusion.

She screamed at Darcus, "Go back! Go back!" But Darcus didn't even turn or acknowledge her. He just kept walking with a satisfied smile on his face. The feeble old mule plodded on down the road. It was then that Prudence realized that she had been banished and she would never see her husband or child again.

As soon as the cart rumbled off the drawbridge, the Duchess whirled and walked triumphantly back to the Great Hall. Her husband was as she had left him. Staring at the floor, he shook his head, perplexed.

As she seated herself with a swish of her skirts, he looked up and asked, "Why, Euphoria? You've sent Lady Prudence on an impossible journey with winter approaching. She could freeze. She could be assaulted, robbed, or murdered. She'll never survive. She is an innocent woman. What has she done to warrant such a punishment?"

"What colour are her eyes, dear husband?"

The Duke paused, "Brown, I think."

"What colour are Sir Frederick's eyes?"

"Brown as well."

"What colour are Verity's eyes?"

"Blue... Oh! I see!"

"Not so innocent after all. And, dear husband, Lady Prudence knows about our precious red flowers of the lake."

"Oh!" the Duke exclaimed. "Then why did you let her go? She will tell!"

"No, my dear, she doesn't know what the flowers do or where they grow. I'm not sure she even knows why she is being punished, because I acted so swiftly. We are safe for now."

"What do you mean, 'for now?'"

"There are two more who know. Do not fret, my husband! I will neutralize them, too!"

But the Duchess had overlooked one not-so-insignificant observer. As she had spun arrogantly and marched out of the Bailey and back into the castle, the scullery boy in dirty grey clothes fastened himself like a fly to the castle wall and watched. Tears ran down his dirty face as he watched the drawbridge raise and the portcullis lower, cutting off his last view of Prudence—the only person who had shown him kindness in the past six years. He wiped his face clear of tears and limped as rapidly as he could toward the stables.

Strangely, the boy Garrod was not terrified of horses, even though Darcus's horse had broken his leg and killed his mother. Garrod knew it was not the horse's doing—only humans were capable of evil.

He hurried to seek help. He went straight to Sir Bennefield and told him what he had seen and heard. Garrod had heard much, for he had still been cleaning up the Great Hall after the noon meal when the Duchess had sent for Prudence. Garrod knew well how to use his insignificance for invisibility. He finished his tale urgently, pleading for the big knight to save his mistress.

Bennefield saw life in simple terms. He nodded briefly, "Of course, let's go. We'll bring your mistress back. Must be some misunderstanding." The friendly giant couldn't conceive of any malicious intent in the incident.

"I can't go!" exclaimed Garrod. "I cannot walk that far. I gimp!"

Bennefield chuckled. "I do not propose we walk, lad. I shall ride my destrier," referring to his warhorse, "and you shall ride my groom's palfrey."

"But I know not how to ride!"

"Ho, ho, ho!" laughed the huge knight. "It's easy, lad, just put one leg on one side and one on the other and hang on!"

Before the stunned boy could figure out an answer to that simple logic, the two were on their way thanks to the friendly gatekeeper. This time, only the sleepy sentries observed the departure and they were only alert to arrivals.

Chapter 14

TREACHERY AFOOT

Far down the road to the south, Prudence had cried herself out. She was numb with cold and so tired and bruised from the rough road and jouncing cart that she felt nothing at all anymore. Her head nodded and she slumped sideways against a large bundle. She lost conscious thought and slept.

Darcus looked back slyly from time to time and when he was sure she had passed out, he pulled the mule and cart off the road. He climbed down and scurried into the bushes. He gave a whistle and was gratified to hear his own horse's answering whinny. A few moments later, his ebony horse trotted down the road. Darcus pulled his steed into the woods and tied him. He then climbed a tree and settled down to wait for fate to take a hand. Anticipating the worst and licking his lips in glee, Darcus watched Prudence's cart, which was visible in the faint moonlight.

He speculated what would happen. He knew Prudence would be hopelessly lost as there were many turns in the road and he had deliberately taken the wrong direction at the crossroads. Would she attempt to go on or go back? Would she wake before morning? Would she be assaulted, robbed, or murdered?

His horse gave a low whinny. Darcus listened and smiled. It seemed he wouldn't have to wait long. He grinned. Two horses cantered down the road.

Then, a young voice announced, "There she is!"

Darcus slid forward on the limb, wondering who had come.

The small horse had a dwarf or a child on its back, but the destrier's rider was, unmistakably, the giant! Darcus scrambled further forward on the branch to listen to their conversation.

"Milady, wake up!"

Prudence stirred. She mumbled, "Don't hurt me! Leave me alone!"

Garrod scrambled into the cart and looked for provisions. He found bread and wine, and handed them to the giant, who pressed the wineskin to Prudence's lips. She roused.

"Sir Bennefield! What are you doing here?"

"We've come to take you back."

"I can't go back! The Duchess has sent me away to get rid of me. Where's Darcus?"

"He's deserted."

"See? It's what she intends. I cannot go back. She'll do something worse."

"Then, what do you propose, Milady? You can't stay here."

Prudence thought for a moment. "The only way I can return is by completing the impossible task she set for me. If I accomplish it and return with laces and velvets or whatever she has on the horrid list, I can see Verity and Frederick again. Is Frederick still alive?"

"Yes, Milady. He's in good hands. If this is the only way, then Garrod and I are at your service." He lowered his voice. "Now, the first thing to do is get out of this isolated backwater and..."

Thud!

"What was that?"

They listened for several minutes. Prudence's heart hammered so loudly she couldn't be sure she could hear anything. Garrod held his breath.

"Never mind," said Bennefield at last. "Let's be gone."

With Lady Prudence on the palfrey and Garrod driving the cart, they turned and headed back up the trail to the crossroads.

Darcus picked himself up off the ground. "Damn branch," he muttered, knowing full well he had edged out too far. Pulling a blanket from his horse, he wrapped himself up tightly and settled to sleep for a while to give the cart, the mule, and the two horses a chance to get well ahead. Then he would ride back to the castle to report to the Duchess that her plan had gone sour. He didn't relish the idea of bearing bad news.

Later the next day, Darcus told his story to the Duchess. He carefully put himself in the best light. The Duchess's reaction was much better than he had hoped. She laughed. He stood perplexed. Was she so drugged by her magic flower potion that she didn't understand?

"Thank you, Darcus, for such good news!"

Is she totally batty? thought Darcus.

"Now I know how to deal with problem number three! You shall tell your story tomorrow in the Great Hall—only this time there will be a few slight changes."

"Yes, Milady!" said Darcus and they both laughed.

The next day in the Great Hall, everyone buzzed with gossip. The Duchess had placed a few hints in just the right ears, and tongues wagged happily throughout the entire meal.

Finally, the Duke brought the room to order and dealt with a number of estate problems. He turned to his wife. "I understand you have a problem in discipline, my dear?"

"Yes. My servant, Darcus."

"Call for Darcus to come forward!"

The crowd buzzed with anticipation, for Darcus was a mean-spirited young man. He had managed to put everyone in trouble in one way or another, and the crowd looked forward to seeing him in trouble. Darcus came up and faced the Duchess with his head lowered and bowed.

"I sent you as escort to Lady Prudence, did I not?"

"Yes, Milady, you did and I did as I was told."

"You did, did you? Then why are you here? Where is Lady Prudence?"

"I travelled with her until well after nightfall when she fell asleep and I did as well. The next I knew, a man was molesting her." The crowd murmured.

"Hush!" said the Duchess to regain attention. "Molesting her? Are you certain?"

"Oh, yes. I heard her say clearly, 'Don't hurt me!'"

"Did you not defend her?"

"Milady, I am not very big, but I did my best. The next I knew, I was on the ground!"

"Ohhh!" murmured the crowd.

"What happened then?" asked the Duchess.

"He pressed a wineskin to her lips to get her drunk and then he said, 'I've come to take you.' She kept saying, 'I cannot!' but he wouldn't listen."

"Why did you not get up and defend her honour?"

"I could not, Milady. He was too big for me to fight. He was better armed and he had another big fellow with him!" The audience gasped.

"Could you identify this scoundrel?"

"Yes, Milady. She called him by name." The crowd leaned forward as one to hear the name of the man who now had Lady Prudence in his clutches.

"Well? What was his name, Darcus?"

"She called him Bennefield, Milady."

Protests of shock and disgust filled the room. No one but the Duchess saw Kailan slip from her seat and swoon in a dead faint under the table.

"Order! Order!" called the Duke.

At last there was quiet.

The Duchess asked, "Do you think, Darcus, that they will have travelled far by now? Would you suggest that we could rescue Lady Prudence?"

"I don't think Lady Prudence would welcome a rescue, Milady," said Darcus slyly.

"Why not?"

"Because she said loudly that she would not come back to the castle. She left quite willingly. In fact, she led the way on horseback."

The Duchess watched as gossip did its work. The crowd buzzed like a disturbed hive. She smiled as she glided smoothly out the doorway on her husband's arm.

By the end of the week, Kailan had left for the convent, and the Duchess had no one to stop her, as she planned how she would turn Verity into a toad.

Chapter 15

THE FRIENDLY WIZARD

Though the wind stirred the limbs of the forest, the pale moon revealed no sign of movement near the castle. It was after curfew and the watchman had long ago checked that the fires were banked, and that all but one of the torches in each passageway had been extinguished.

Closer to the Keep, if anyone had been there, one could have seen a faint glimmer moving up from one window to the next. Heavily cloaked, a black figure mounted the circular staircase so smoothly that the only movement visible was the ripple of the cloak's train trailing ever upward.

The figure continued to glide along the corridor without a sound. It stopped by the Garret door. With a whisper, the door opened and the black-cloaked menace towered over the slight figure asleep on the cot. The squeak of the door hadn't roused the sleeper; had she woken at that moment, she would have been shocked to see the scowl of hatred on the beautiful face above her.

Pausing to study the sleeping girl, the cloaked woman brought out a pair of scissors from her sack and snipped a lock of the brown hair, which she returned to her bag. Careful not to drip any wax from her candle, the woman softly exited the room.

Verity woke with a start in her small bedchamber. What was the sound that woke her from her troubled dreams? She felt the damp of her tears on her pillow, but lay quietly, listening for the sound to repeat. Her heart pounded as she identified the distant screech of a bat—or perhaps someone waking with a nightmare in the echoing castle. Had she heard the wings of a night bird or... a door hinge? Yes! The hinge of her door squeaked exactly like that!

She flew to the door, opened it, and looked down the passage. There was no one in sight, but she could see the soft, retreating glow of a candle illuminating the curved wall of the stairwell. Someone had opened her door to see if she were sleeping. Why would anyone care about what she was doing in the middle of the night?

The glow on the wall faded. A cool breeze chilled her. She shut her door and crept back to bed. She turned her pillow to the dry side and pulled the covers tightly over herself for warmth.

She thought and she remembered. A fortnight ago, someone had opened her door in the night and had left it open. She had awakened to a chilling draft in her room and the sound of wind in the passages moaning like a ghost. Had a ghost opened her door? She turned on her side in disgust at her own imagination. A ghost would be more welcome than the thought that someone was spying on her as she slept.

Why would anyone be interested in a skinny adolescent female with mousy hair, big eyes, and no prospects? She pondered her situation thoughtfully and remembered her dream. All her dreams began the same way. She would be looking for her mother in the castle, in the woods, in the meadow, and in the market. She could still recall the frantic feeling. Then each dream would change. Sometimes she would be in the convent and Kailan would be there. Sometimes she would travel to a great city and become lost in the markets. Sometimes she would meet a mysterious stranger in the woods and he would carry her away on his great destrier. Then, just as the dreams would become pleasant, the Duchess would appear suddenly and scream, "You're just a toad! You have no need for friends or pretty dresses or handsome strangers." And Verity would shrink, her eyes would bulge, and she'd croak.

"That's who it is! The Duchess! She thinks I told my mother about her rotten flowers."

Verity thought back to that awful day five years ago when her mother had left. How she had cried when she learned that her mother was gone. But one day soon after, her father had recovered and returned to the castle.

She thought, *He told me he would find mother and bring her back, and he told me the Wizard would look after me. There's been no word for years. If it weren't for Violet, I'm sure the Duchess would make me live in the pond with the rest of the toads.*

Dawn slipped over the windowsill and rested on the long wavy hair and the long curling lashes. Verity slept until the breakfast horn sounded. She brushed her hair, washed her face, slipped on her plain brown dress, and headed for the Great Hall, just as she had for the past five years.

Then one morning, Verity noticed that she was once again running out of her supply of soapwort. She passed the small brown lump under her nose.

She thought, *I love the fragrance of it—like woods on a rainy day. I wonder how mother learned to make it and what ingredient makes it smell so fresh. The regular, conventional soap is whiter, but it doesn't smell nearly as nice. I must see Agatha in the Scullery.*

Thinking of old Agatha, Verity reflected on the curious incident some weeks earlier when she discovered that it wasn't Agatha who knew the secret ingredient, but Agatha's source, the Wizard. Verity had been running to meet Violet in the rose garden to collect petals for the castle. Passing the Scullery, she'd glimpsed the Wizard talking to Agatha. He'd had his large black raven on his shoulder. She'd stopped and stared. The Wizard poured a dark brown powder into Agatha's bowl while he talked to her in a low voice. Agatha nodded and spoke. Verity heard her say, "…misses her mother, but…" and when the Wizard spoke again, he used her name, "Verity." They had turned away without seeing her and Verity had joined Violet in the garden.

Verity never feared the Wizard and his renowned magic. Before her father had left to find her mother, he had assured her that the Wizard would look after her.

"Remember, dear Verity, if you are ever ill, send for the Wizard. Ask Agatha to fetch him. If you are ever afraid, go to the Wizard. Follow the fork to the left in the woods. It will take you directly to him."

Brushing her hair, Verity thought back to the first time she had taken the left fork. Verity and Violet had taken their new tutor, Brother Delancey, to the woods. He was a student of plants, which he illustrated. While he and Violet were examining the wood violets, Verity slipped down the left path, running as fast as she could until she smelled smoke. She slowed and then tiptoed around a big boulder in the path and there was the most enchanting cottage sitting in a bright patch of sunlight. She stood and gazed at the smoke curling lazily from its chimney indicating the occupant was at home. A hand touched her shoulder and she jumped. She looked up into the twinkling, faded blue eyes of the Wizard.

A smile played around his mouth as if he couldn't speak for grinning. She grinned back and they both laughed out loud, just for the fun of it.

The Wizard threw his soft brown cape back over his shoulder and sat down on a log. "Now you know where I am, my dear, do you need my help?"

"No, sir, I was curious." She blushed.

The raven flew down to the Wizard's shoulder and cocked his head. Verity laughed again. "So the raven belongs to you?"

"Belongs? Precisely? No. If anything, I would say that I belong to him. His name is Rothko and he definitely belongs to himself." The Wizard reached over and tweaked the bird's beak. The great wings flapped in protest, but the bird remained on his shoulder. The Wizard continued, "There isn't anything that goes on in the forest or the castle that this black rogue doesn't know about. He tells me you're out of your mother's special hair soap."

Verity's eyes widened, "Is he magical?"

The Wizard laughed. "You might say that. When you need more of it, just ask old Agatha in the scullery. Now, should you be returning?"

"Oh dear! I forgot Violet and Brother Fancy. They'll think I'm lost. I'd better go."

"Brother Fancy?" asked the Wizard with a chuckle.

Verity backed up the path as she rapidly explained, "Actually, his name is Delancey—he's a monk and our tutor. He's rather slow to catch onto our pranks, but he loves to draw plants and he's rather sweet. I wouldn't want him to worry."

"Then don't take him to the flowers by the lake," said the Wizard sternly.

Verity stopped. Her eyes widened, "N-no sir, I won't."

How did he know? she wondered, taking another step backward.

The Wizard raised his arms. "Action, dust. Return she must!"

A bright light flashed.

Verity was back at the fork in the path. She was breathing hard, as if she'd been running. Off on the other fork to her left, she could see Brother Fancy drawing an intricate fern. Violet was playing with a beetle and watching the monk.

Verity took a deep breath, smoothed her skirts, and said to Violet, "The sun is almost overhead. We'd better return to the castle, or your mother will be worried and we wouldn't want to worry her."

Thoughts of such consequences crossed the two faces in quick succession.

Violet turned back up the path and Verity, after helping Brother Fancy gather his art materials, followed her. It was an uphill walk back to the castle. Verity grinned to herself and wished she could have a little of the Wizard's magical "action dust."

Putting down her hairbrush, Verity smiled, enjoying the memory of first meeting the Wizard. *Perhaps I'll just see Agatha,* she thought. *Rothko probably already knows and has passed the word.* She left her chamber to begin the day.

Chapter 16

TWO SCAMPS PUNISHED

The sun was overhead, but little of it lit the gloomy hallways of the castle. Violet and Verity dashed down the passage at full speed, whipping around the corner to the Great Hall. They were in no danger of running into anyone; they were dreadfully late.

They paused before the entrance by the great bowls of water—almost empty now—to splash water on their faces and hands. Then, hunching down, they tried to make themselves as inconspicuous as possible and, following a server, they crept to their places at the long table under the eye of the Duchess. That Lady was turned to the Duke who was lavishing compliments on her as usual. No one paid the girls any attention, so they started to eat, whispering hopes that the Duchess had not noticed their tardiness.

Violet mopped up the meat gravy with her bread. With a sigh of pleasure, she savoured the flavour and closed her eyes. Verity's attention was drawn from her pewter plate. Ignoring the savoury stew, her eyes narrowed as she watched Brother Fancy, who sat across the table, just above the salt. He too was enjoying his stew, but Verity was certain the pleasure of it was not enough to make a monk chuckle. She had caught him glancing at Violet and herself, and then shaking like jelly with mirth. The corners of his mouth widened in a grin, and the gravy dripped down his chin as he tried to eat and laugh simultaneously.

Verity poked Violet sharply. Violet missed her mouth and jabbed gravy into her cheek.

"This time we are the victims," Verity whispered.

Her friend wiped her cheek and followed Verity's gaze to the still-chuckling monk. He looked up at the blue and violet eyes full of awareness and burst out laughing at the full impact of his revenge. The priest, who was sitting next to the monk, passed him a startled look and then glanced at the girls. Dawning comprehension passed across his face. He leaned forward and asked for the salt. The monk obliged while he tried to sober his face. The priest murmured a question too low for Verity to hear. The monk replied and the two men laughed in unison.

The bookkeeper then asked what was so amusing and the mirth began to swell like wind-whipped waves on the lake.

Violet bowed her head close to Verity's. "So he intended to make us late."

"Yes," breathed Verity. "He finally caught on that we were pretending to be stupid."

Violet made a face. "Well, it worked. I didn't care how dumb he thought we were. We got out of a lot of extra work."

Guffaws broke out at the next table. Verity knew it was only a matter of minutes before the Duchess found out their ruse. "That's why he switched to botany. He knows we hate figures and love plants."

Violet's eyebrows rose. "Brother Fancy deliberately made us think this was an easy copying assignment—"

Verity's eyes narrowed, "—and left the hardest one on his desk so we wouldn't see it until it was too late to protest."

"We should have left it unfinished and come to dinner. Better to endure Brother Fancy's wrath than the wrath—of Mother!"

"The Duchess!" Verity quietly chorused in agreement.

Slowly, they turned their sober faces to the head table. The hard, grey eyes of the Duchess pinned them in place for a long moment. There was no defying that look. They shrank in humility. The Duke's attention was also aroused, and he looked at the girls, fixing his attention on Verity.

"We'll be shovelling manure," said Violet regretfully, and pushed away her plate.

Verity pulled at her skirt and tucked her legs under the bench out of sight. The expression on the Duke's face as he stared at her made her feel even more uneasy. She had sprouted again and her skirts were too short. She thought that was a worse problem than shoveling shit.

Dinner was altogether too short and announcements even shorter, especially for two girls awaiting certain punishment. They hung their heads in shame rather than face the glare of the Duchess. All too soon, they were lined up with Brother Fancy in front of the head table.

"Brother Delancey," began the Duke, "we understand there has been a problem in the schoolroom. Would you explain to us the charade that has led to such embarrassment?"

Brother Fancy adopted a humble face. "When I assumed the duties of Brother Cerric, who had tutored your young ladies for several years, there was no opportunity to converse with him about the position. He had already departed, you see."

"Sounds like he's dead," whispered Violet and giggled.

The Duchess snapped, "Violet!" Violet sobered.

Brother Fancy cleared his throat. "My colleague, Brother Cerric, had left notes sufficient to inform me of the lessons accomplished, and an outline of their expected education." The Duke nodded in agreement.

The monk coughed slightly into his hand. "What Brother Cerric failed to do was inform me as to the abilities and character of the two—ahem—young ladies." He nodded at Violet and Verity, who expectantly wondered whether he'd help them save face or hand them shovels.

He shook his head and the one curl abandoned in the middle of his pate wobbled.

"Unfortunately," he sighed, "I naturally assumed the slowness they feigned was real. They are females after all."

Three pairs of eyes frowned. Three mouths pursed narrowly. The Duke just nodded again. Verity looked at the Duchess and thought she would see a glimmer of hope. Verity knew the Duchess was determined to see her daughter well educated in her letters, which was against the custom for girls.

Brother Fancy continued, "Because they appeared dense and dull-witted, I explained lessons most clearly, cut lessons in half, and gave them extended periods of time to accomplish their assignments."

The Duchess's mouth began to twitch. She glanced at the girls, met Verity's eye, and became stern again.

Brother Fancy looked at the girls as though he still couldn't believe he'd been duped. "It wasn't until their pranks became quite elaborate that I began to suspect they were more intelligent than I had believed."

"Pranks?" asked the Duke, intrigued.

"Yes!" The monk cleared his throat again and resumed. "I had sat in something sticky, been stung by a bee, and slipped on a greased floor, all without suspicion. But then..."

"Then?" prompted the Duke, fascinated.

"Then came the day I tripped and fell into horseshit."

This statement was met with complete silence.

"I had failed to inspire them to add their figures. 'No purpose,' they said, and I could see their point, so I explained the importance was related to running the estate. 'How?' they asked. 'What did nine plus eighteen have to do with cookery, or jousting, or the care of horses?' I most eagerly leaped on the economy of the stable. I reflect now if I had chosen kitchens, I would have landed in the stew! I explained how the cost of so many horses plus their food and care was a debit on the castle's books. 'So what?' they said. 'How many horses were there to cause such a worry?' they asked. I confessed I knew not. 'Then let's go count them, Brother Fancy,' they said."

He blushed, realizing he had revealed their pet name for him.

"They said, 'you always insist we be accurate in our figures and yet we do not know how many horses our castle is responsible for!'" Brother Fancy paused and put his clutched hand to his mouth. "And so we went to the stable to count horses. It was not very clean that day. One stable boy apologized and told me there was an order from the Duke not to clean the stable that Wednesday."

"I gave no such order," frowned the Duke.

The monk raised his hand. "I know, I know, it was contrived by them. Inside the stable, the girls split up. While one flirted with a squire, the other pulled a horse's tail. I pulled her back before he bucked and placed her on some clean straw. I turned to help the other who was tiptoeing across the piss-filled floor. I could hear the first lass counting the horses aloud when she shrieked. I spun around and stepped quickly to the rescue, tripped on a pitchfork... and you know the rest." He looked up at the Duke and Duchess's frowning faces.

"It was this prank—so elaborate—that made me realize how clever these two young ladies are. I rigged an assignment to trap them into being late for dinner—a minor revenge under the circumstances. I wanted them to be found out, you see, and em-barrassed and," he raised his voice, "possibly brought to justice?"

"It worked!" said the Duchess. "Leave it to me, and from now on Brother Delancey, lay on the work!"

"Yes, Milady!"

"Dismissed," said the Duchess.

The monk waddled out on his sandaled feet. The Duke and Duchess stared down at the girls. Verity pulled her skirt and bent her knees to cover her feet. She hunched her shoulders to ease her straining bodice.

The Duchess snapped, "Stand straight, Verity!"

Verity straightened. The Duke's look travelled from her ankles to her bodice. She blushed.

The Duchess bit her lip. "You are both forbidden to go to the Fair. And there will be no falconry for a fortnight. See if you can apply yourselves to catch up on your lessons. If not, these restrictions will be extended another fortnight."

Verity felt the Duke's stare and trembled as if she were naked. The Duchess took note of the trembling and traced the direction of her husband's gaze. The Duchess's eyelids lowered slightly and a hint of green clouded her grey eyes.

"It has come to my attention," she began in a soft, syrupy voice, "that you have grown, dear Verity. I'm sure Violet can spare a gown or two."

Violet's gaze rose quickly from the floor. She smiled. "I have a lovely light blue gown I've outgrown. I'm sure we can take it in for Verity. Blue would look lovely on her."

Verity did not acknowledge her friend's enthusiasm. She knew better. She kept her eyes cast down and thought, *Here it comes.*

There was a long silence. She raised her eyes to the Duchess, who smiled. Verity's eyes widened. They looked enormous in her dainty face.

"Perhaps," murmured the Duchess, "but we must be practical, dear daughter. With no mother or father to watch out for our dear Verity, we must see to it that her gowns give her long wear. So dye it brown—no! This time dark peasant green—a suitable colour for our little toad! Ha, ha, ha, ha, ha!"

Chapter 17

AN APPARITION

In the dim predawn light, Verity slipped on her green dress and gave it a tug. She looked down in dismay at her narrow feet and ankles. Oh, no! She'd grown yet again!

I wonder what ugly dress the Duchess can create this time, she thought. Actually she didn't mind the green. She preferred it to the brown, but she'd never let the Duchess know that! She was fond of referring to her green dress as "pond scum" when she thought the Duchess could hear and Violet could not. It always made the Duchess smirk, but comments such as that could hurt Violet, and Verity would never willingly do that.

Verity hurried down to Violet's chamber. It was a distinct contrast to her own poor Garret. Violet's big carved posts and draft-protecting drapery provided security, like the security Verity had felt as a child with her mother's arms around her. She turned into the passage that led to the Tower room and stopped short, as thoughts of her mother fogged her purpose. She could see her mother's gentle brown eyes. She imagined the musical cadence of her speech.

Then she thought she saw her mother ahead in the dim passage, glowing with a golden luminosity. Long, flaxen hair floated like an aura around her smiling face. Verity took a step closer. She thought she might be seeing a ghost because she could faintly see through the image. But, she dismissed it because she felt no cold draft and certainly no fear.

"I miss you, Mother," she whispered.

"I love you," said the apparition, but then...

A maid passed behind Verity in the passage to Violet's room. The flame on the servant's candle flickered. But the woman, sheltering the flame, trudged on and did not notice Verity, standing still in the dark, much less the glowing apparition.

Verity quickly turned back. There was still a slight glow, but no features could be distinguished.

"Mother?" She could hear a slight murmur. "Mother! I can't hear you."

"Verity…"

"Yes!" she answered.

"Sssssoon…"

"Mother, are you de—a ghost?"

Then she saw the hint of a smile on her mother's transparent face.

"Ssooonnnnnn," said the glow and faded.

Verity walked over and stood in the spot. She felt warm.

It was not a ghost, she thought, and smiled. *Something good will happen soon—I'm sure of it. I must tell the Wizard.* She hurried to Violet's chamber. There was much to do before she could seek out the Wizard.

Chapter 18

PROSPECTS

Verity ran lightly through the passageway to Violet's chamber. She knocked on the heavy door. Violet opened it and hastily pulled her friend inside.

"The letter has arrived," Violet gushed. "I heard them talking about it last night. I am frantic with excitement. My whole future is about to be decided."

Verity took hold of her hands. "What does it say? What do your parents say?"

"I just know that it has come, and none too soon. I am almost beyond the negotiating age for marriage. Perhaps they will tell me at midday. My stomach! I am so nervous."

Verity pulled her friend's hand. "Come. We must break our fast and then you will feel better."

The girls hurried to the kitchen for a sweet bun and watered wine. They discussed the knights of the castle as they ate.

"Of course, Antonio has no prospects. He is so lazy," contemplated Violet sadly, aloud.

"But he is handsome—and such a flirt," smiled Verity. "What about Raimond?"

"Likewise, no prospects. He's not lazy, but he's not very ambitious either."

"Albertus? He must be doing well. He looks prosperous, and I've heard he has some land."

"But he's so…" faltered Violet, with a wrinkled face and closed eyes.

Verity laughed. "I know, dear friend, I wouldn't want to wake up and look at that, either."

They entered the schoolroom. Brother Delancey arose and

approached Violet. He put his hand on her shoulder and looked kindly into her eyes.

"Violet, your parents request that you meet them before dinner in the Salon. The Duchess reminds you both to be early. It doesn't look seemly for you to arrive late and delay dinner for all. Every minute waiting for the head table is uncomfortable for growling empty stomachs."

No doubt he is thinking of his own, thought Verity.

"This was explained to you when you were moved up to the head table. Nothing can begin until the head table is seated. You must realize…"

Violet raised a hand, protesting, "I know, I know. I will be there."

The Brother moved back to his books. "Good, good. Then let us begin. The sooner we begin, the sooner you can begin your copy and the earlier you may be dismissed for your consultation with the Duchess. It wouldn't do at all for you to keep her waiting and…"

"Brother Fancy," said Violet sharply, "stop dithering. You didn't mention a consultation!"

"Yes, yes, of course I did. That is why you must be there early and be sure you are, so we can start dinner."

"Brother," said Violet again, "a consultation?"

He looked up puzzled. "Yes, didn't I say? The Duke and Duchess want you to come early to discuss the letter."

"Ahhhhh!" sighed Violet.

"Yes, indeed," said the monk, and then more quietly he added, "you are growing up, Violet." Then he stirred himself. "Our lesson today…"

Sometime later, Brother Fancy tiptoed out of the room. For some minutes no sound broke the stillness except for the scratching of two quills as the girls copied the assigned Latin text.

At last, Verity put down her quill. "I shall miss you, Violet."

"But I shan't go without you!" protested Violet.

"You will have no choice and neither will I. I shall join Kailan if I can get into the nunnery. Perhaps they would be pleased to have my skills in Latin."

"I shall ask Mother and Father to supply you with a dowry!"

Surprise and hope flashed across Verity's face and then reality set her mouth firmly.

"I know," said Violet softly. "It wouldn't be much. They are not exactly generous to you, but maybe you could live near me?"

Verity smiled. "Maybe. For now, just think about yourself. You have the right to refuse if you hate the man they choose. Remember that."

Violet rubbed her forehead. "I know, but they could make life unbearable if I thwart them. Especially Mother. I know. I've tried." She shook her head as she recalled trying to persuade the Duchess to allow Verity to wear her old blue silk all those years ago.

"Let's finish our lesson. I'll wait near the Salon in the alcove while you meet your parents and later, let's take our birds out. The air will do you good and we can talk freely away from the castle."

Violet smiled and they moved their quills carefully over their pages. Brother Delancey grunted with satisfaction when he returned to find the girls working quietly. *They are growing up,* he thought. *Soon I will return to the monastery.* He smiled with satisfaction and then a sad expression stole quietly into his eyes as he watched his two pupils. In spite of himself, he had grown quite fond of them.

The girls washed ink from their fingers and splashed water on their faces. They slowly walked along the passage to the Salon.

"I shall wait here for you. Let me know when you are to enter the Hall." Verity sat down on the bottom of the three steps to the Salon and drew her skirts closely around her.

"Wish me luck," whispered Violet, and opened the door. Verity could see a glimpse of the Duchess between Violet and the edge of the doorway. The Duchess's set expression relaxed as she saw her daughter and she immediately raised her eyebrow as she spied Verity on the step. The door closed, leaving Verity in the near dark of the dusky passage.

Time passed like a slug. Verity contemplated her own future. Perhaps if she could acquire a small dowry, she could marry a knight and they could live at Violet's new home. She thought about the knights. She regretted her own poor flirting techniques. She knew none of them were attracted to her scrawny body. No lingering glance looked into her eyes. Her best flirting consisted of exchanging quips. She thought about the unfortunate Albertus. He couldn't help his weak chin and pockmarked face. She wondered if he were a kind man. He was acquiring wealth steadily. With wealth came power. He must be fairly clever. Maybe he would age well. She tried to remember his mouth. Was it generous and soft or hard and resentful? She couldn't remember, because she hardly looked at him and felt guilty that she had been so repulsed by an unfortunate human visage.

Lost in thought, she was startled when Darcus spoke.

"You'll never hear through that door, Toadie. Better hop to it and let me by or I'll have you fried for supper."

Verity sprang up. With revulsion, she flattened herself against the wall's cold stone. She curled into the wall to protect herself, but Darcus trapped her against the wall with his body, as he clutched her bum and he licked her neck. With a gruff groan of terror, Verity broke away from him and ran down the passage, leaving him laughing like an eel.

It was now impossible to wait for Violet by the Salon. Verity made her way through the arriving dinner crowd toward the kitchen to eat with Agatha. It was only later that she remembered that Darcus had had another letter in his hand.

Chapter 19

HUNTING

Agatha held Verity's trembling body with strong, comforting arms. "There, there, chile. Wot is it?"

"Darcus!" Verity shuddered and wiped her neck yet again.

"Well, ye'll miss ye dinner. Juss eat with yur ol' Aggie here in the kitchen. Later, ye can tell the ol' crone ye were ill. But don' say a word to 'er about Darcus. The ol' bird won't hear a word against her dark chickee."

"Why does she like him? He... slithers!"

With a fond look, Agatha gave Verity a mince pie. "It takes a snake to do the terrible deeds she dreams up. Jes' 'member. Keep to the light 'n' avoid the Darcus!" Agatha chuckled at her own wit.

Verity felt better after the food. She retrieved her cloak from the Garret and pulled on her boots before she made her way to the mews. The stables were quiet. People had not returned from dinner. Verity sat on a stump to wait for Violet and hoped she hadn't missed any crucial announcements. The falconer was pleased to see her when he returned from dinner and briskly organized the palfreys, grooms, and dogs. The peregrines and goshawks began to cry out with excitement as they heard the dogs and anticipated the outing.

It was some time later that Violet arrived and she had forgotten her boots. A servant was dispatched to fetch them.

"What did your parents say about the letters? What do they plan to do?" asked Verity. Violet looked excited and Verity felt smothered with curiosity.

"Later!" cautioned Violet, glancing at the falconer's inquisitive face.

As soon as they were riding on the wide path, side-by-side,

Violet began. "There seems to be animosity toward Father. The letters are not very cordial and they suggest they will only entertain negotiations because of my Grandfather's legacy. This is why it has taken so long. Another letter has arrived signifying agreement to listen. Mother is furious. She told Father it's his fault that she isn't received at court. I had no idea that we were shunned at court because of political undercurrents, did you?"

Verity shook her head. "What are your choices?"

"We must travel. I am to be paraded like a mare who's taught to bow and scrape. It's humiliating!"

Verity glanced around to be sure they were not being overheard. "No one could resist you, Violet. You are beautiful and clever. Suitors will compete for you once they see you."

Violet turned to her friend. "I couldn't bear being on parade without your support," she smiled. "That's the good part of my news. I refused to go unless you come too! Properly attired, of course! I told Mother I would not cooperate unless they agreed."

"You said that?" gasped Verity, pulling on her reins in surprise. The palfrey stopped. She urged him on again. "What did the Duchess say to that?"

"Quote?"

"Yes, quote."

"Mother said, 'As long as the toad remains as invisible as possible, and refrains from croaking, she can come.' So you see, dear Verity, we may both succeed yet!"

Verity returned to the most pressing question. "Who are your choices?"

"First, there is a large estate of lands north and adjacent to us. I was informed that the owner is a Baron, wealthy beyond his properties, experienced, well travelled, and a widower. It seems his one child left home and never returned. Mother assures me he will die soon and would leave me a wealthy widow with an open choice of further suitors."

"But what if he should live long? Marry an old man? Ugh! What other choice is there?"

Violet guided her palfrey around a boulder on the path. "The second is our Knight, Sir Albertus, who will inherit lands in England and is willing—but we would have to move to England."

A pall of silence fell on the two as they contemplated permanent separation. "They say the rainy English climate is kind to the skin," ventured Violet with a sigh.

"Then why is he so...?" Verity grinned. "But it doesn't do much for the rest of the face." The girls laughed. It felt better to laugh even at someone's expense when they were considering such daunting prospects.

They were nearing the meadow. Violet slowed her palfrey. "The third option seems the nicest, but the most difficult. The Noble's son is young and not yet promised in marriage. The Noble was a good friend of Grandfather's. His first son was killed in battle. Their estate is near Paris. They are well connected at Court."

"Oh, Violet! That would be wonderful. You would be such a graceful addition to Court."

"That is good of you to say. You are a good friend, Verity. There is bad feeling, however, on the Noble's part. He is the one who kept Mother from Court. He has finally agreed, reluctantly, to... look at me." She gulped against her dry throat.

Verity nodded. "I see. What chance might you have if you could be seen at Court?" She looked at Violet. "What about the Prince himself?"

Violet bit her lip, then looked up toward the falconer who was waiting with their birds in the meadow. "Le Marquis de Cortelaide spread rumours at Court about Mother, claiming her to be an evil sorceress who eats flowers and casts spells, so... probably no chance at all."

Violet urged her palfrey up the last rise and Verity followed. The girls greeted the falconer and took charge of their birds. Violet's peregrine was especially excited but she calmed him with soothing sounds. Verity matched Violet's calm voice as she said, "We will talk again later. For now, let us enjoy our hunt."

Violet sat erect holding her peregrine on her heavy leather

glove. Sounds rose up the hill from the beaters and their dogs. With rustles and squawks, the quarry rose flapping into the sky. Watching the chief falconer for his signal, Violet undid the ties on her bird's hood. The bird trembled with excitement. The falconer raised his arm. Violet removed the hood and the bird sprang from her wrist with a mighty beat of wings and rose into the sky.

Violet urged her horse forward and gave chase, watching the peregrine as it soared above its quarry, which was a brightly coloured mallard. Violet measured the landscape and altered her course to the site of the kill. It was easier to lure back her bird if she was positioned well. The mounted grooms followed her.

Verity shaded her eyes against the afternoon sun as she watched the soaring peregrine. It abruptly dove, hitting the prey with jolting force. Verity expelled a deep breath she hadn't even realized she was holding. It was awesome to think of the peregrine's power; moments earlier, that power had been contained as it sat docilely on her friend's wrist. As exciting as it was to watch, Verity didn't envy her friend the prestigious bird. To Verity, her own smaller goshawk hen was far more challenging. Once her turn came and her bird took off, she would have to ride hard and fast to keep up. Because the goshawk pursued its prey from behind, her mistress became part of the chase. Verity thought, *It's much better being part of it rather than just watching.*

Hours later, their party returned to the castle with a brace of birds and rabbits. The flushed cheeks and sparkling eyes of the two girls drew the Duke's mouth in a happy curve. Supper was such a pleasant affair that they all lingered over their wine and listened to the minstrel singing familiar airs to the accompaniment of his harp. In the midst of a love ballad, the Duchess saw the Duke's eyes lingering curiously on Verity. She abruptly called an end to the entertainment and pulled the Duke off to bed.

After hours of afternoon pursuit in the strong sunshine and a satisfying meal, Verity was drowsy and ready to shut her eyes. When she passed the watchman on his way down the stairs, she

knew the fires were already covered and it would be chilly preparing for bed. She hurried the process and pulled the covers
tightly around her. She fell asleep imagining what might happen
on the journey with Violet. "Bless Violet for including me in her
adventure," she smiled as she fell into the soft sensation of sleep.

Later that night, when the wind moaned through the cracks
in the castle, the Duchess woke to the moans of her husband
having the first of many nightmares.

Chapter 20

THWARTED

Weeks of frantic activity passed before the Duchess was prepared to take her household on the road. As her daughter's companion, Verity needed proper garments of good quality cloth appropriate for a lady, yet the Duchess supervised every fitting to be sure the quality did not make Verity overly attractive. It would not do at all to have Verity attract the suitors.

Of course, the Duchess restricted the entire wardrobe to a practical green and, of course, Verity pretended to be disappointed. And so, by maintaining the charade, Verity held on to her dignity and let the Duchess believe she was successful in humiliating her.

As much food as possible was prepared in advance: plenty of pies and many loaves of bread. It was awkward to cook enroute. Weapons and bedding, dishes and clothing, cooking pots and candles—the carts and litters filled rapidly. At last, the horn sounded. Into the Bailey swept the Duchess pulling on her gloves, her eyes assessing the entourage. With a grim smile, she gave the signal and, mounting her black steed, she led the way through the gate slightly ahead of her husband. Leather straps creaked, horses whinnied, dogs barked, children shouted farewells, and slowly the parade left the castle grounds.

Violet and Verity were fairly close to the front and were spared the clouds of dust that rose from the carts. The pace of the caravan was naturally slow and frustrating to eager spirits.

"Fergus trembles in frustration almost as much as I do," complained Violet about her horse.

"Dolphus is restless too," said Verity, patting her palfrey, "but we were warned that we would be travelling at the pace of the slowest and those carts are slow."

Violet reached down and twisted the hair of Fergus's mane.

"I just wish some of us could gallop ahead and find our first stopping place."

"I know, Violet, but splitting up would weaken the caravan and our carts would be vulnerable to thieves. Think of your gowns!"

They plodded along in silence for a time then Violet said, "I wonder how old the Baron is," referring to the wealthy suitor who was a widower.

"Too old. The story goes that his son left home many years ago," answered Verity.

"Mother says that's fortunate, for the sooner he dies, the sooner I'll be rich."

"Which would you rather have? Riches or a young husband?"

"Both!" declared Violet.

The sound of the girls' laughter on the breeze made the Duke look back. He sighed, and then as he was out of earshot of the girls, he said, "I wonder how old Sir Rudolph is, my dear."

"The older, the better!" snapped his wife. "Then no one will question my spell once they are married."

"What will you accomplish with your spell?"

"His death, naturally, or unnaturally, depending on your point of view. Then Violet will inherit."

"What about his son?"

"That is a point to negotiate in the marriage contract, of course. He can't expect to get a lovely young wife and then leave her penniless. There is a good site by that stream. Call a halt. We'll stop there for our meal."

Setting up camp and serving food took far too long to suit the Duchess. While in view of the servants, the Duchess whipped several kitchen help as a lesson to all to be more efficient. Even the Duke winced and he tried to calm his wife's temper by distracting her.

Eventually, camp was struck and they moved on with renewed effort to reach the Baron's castle before dark. A steady rise in land took more effort from travellers already weary from the day's journey. Many hours later, there was a break in the trees ahead and they came into a clearing above a cliff. Below was a view of a large valley.

The Duchess called Violet to come forward to see Baron von Balford's castle facing the same view just ahead. "We have arrived, dear Violet."

Violet looked at the crumbling stone of the old castle and her face clouded in disappointment. She exchanged a look with her father. He did not look impressed either. It was in obvious disrepair and the surroundings most neglected. But the Duchess looked quite elated. She smiled with satisfaction and looked at Violet. "Why the long face, my daughter?"

"It's horrible!"

The Duchess laughed. "Do not distress yourself. Just follow me. This will be like taking sweetmeats from a baby," and she urged her stallion forward.

Their reception inside the Bailey was cool and indifferent. The Duke, Duchess, and both girls were ushered directly into the Salon where the old Baron was warming himself by a meagre fire.

The Duchess was quickly disappointed. The old Baron was a bitter man, but certainly not lacking in his senses. He neglected his property because he had no money to care for it and was in fact only interested in the possible dowry from Violet to bolster his fortunes. When he saw how repulsed the young girl was by his frizzy white hair and protruding gut, he suggested that he would marry Violet to give her his good name, but that she wouldn't be obliged to live with him. And he laughed.

Never one to hold her tongue, the Duchess—revolted by the poor food they were served—asked about the extent of his lands.

"As far as I can see, and my eyesight is excellent," was his response.

Encouraged by this, she continued to probe, but when she mentioned his son, the interview ended in disaster. The old Baron ranted on about his ungrateful child, expressed hope never to see him again, and worked himself into a rage, saying, "He won't return except to claim his inheritance." When asked where his son was, he said, "Probably watching from a tree, waiting for me to die, so he can have it all." He stormed out of the hall, purple in the face, hitting a servant on the way.

Violet looked close to tears. Verity put her hand on her friend's arm in consolation and watched the Duchess, whose mouth was tight with fury. After a moment, the Duchess said harshly, "To bed, girls. We start out at dawn. This is a waste of effort. He will regret trying to manipulate me!"

Violet and Verity obeyed at once. The Duke looked uneasy and ordered guards for the night. Long before dawn, the Duchess had everyone up and moving by torchlight; they were glad to be out of the mouldy rooms. They were already on the road when the sun paled the sky.

Sweet buns were passed along the caravan as they moved and thirst was ignored. There was no grumbling. Such was the relief to be gone from the Baron's castle. Again they climbed. Carts were pushed as well as pulled up the steep road. At the peak of a steep rise, some stopped to rest and looked back over the hill toward the castle. Ominously, a thin trail of black smoke rose from within the castle walls. It thickened and a tongue of orange could be seen. The cart drivers shouted alarm.

Well ahead, the Duchess smiled and repeated her order to be sent down the line. "Keep moving!"

On the last rise of the road, before the descent, Verity and Violet could see a large spreading cloud of smoke. Violet shuddered and tears trickled down her cheeks. "The poor old man. I hope no one was hurt."

Verity's eyes rested on the Duchess, who looked self-satisfied and even pleased.

"Don't waste your sympathy, dear daughter," she said. "It gives the man something to do!" Then, she turned to the other gawkers watching the smoke. "Move on! Move on! We have a long way to go!"

Chapter 21

FAIRIES AND BEARS

Well after midday, they camped next to a stream of fresh sweet water. A proper meal and shelters were ordered. They stayed there for the night. Fresh air lent appetite, and a kindly moon looked down on them that night. The next day went smoothly.

By the third day, everyone was accustomed to saddle sores and two meals a day. The caravan made better distance and the pace was faster, because the road had levelled out. They followed the stream, which widened gradually to a river. It made pleasant, cool gurgles and offered occasional refreshment as the day grew warmer. By the time they stopped for the day, the heat was muggy, insects hovered, and tempers were frayed. That night, the low rumbling of thunder brought an uneasy feeling to the camp. Grooms stayed close to the horses, murmuring soothing sounds, but the horses were still restless.

Violet and Verity whispered in the dark. It was too hot to sleep. In their lean-to, the Duchess's maid was snoring peacefully.

"Look, Verity, there are the fairies! They're dancing beside the river."

Verity pushed herself up on her elbow. "Agatha told me that if I could ever catch a fairy, it would just look like a bug, but not to be fooled. It's a fairy, all the same. She told me not to let it go until I make a wish, then wait until it lights three more times. I could use a wish. Let's go capture a fairy!"

Violet sat up and looked around in the dark. "What about Mother?" she whispered.

Verity wrapped her blanket around herself and over her head. "Do it like this. No one will see with these dark blankets over our night shifts." She tiptoed out of the shelter in her bare feet. The deep grass was cool with dew.

Violet struggled to follow. The moon gave little light as they came out from under the trees where their shelter had been placed. A thickening layer of cloud dimmed the stars.

Slowly, they moved toward the river away from the sleeping caravan. A watchman was snoring to their left. It was easy to circle away from him.

Verity stopped abruptly.

Violet bumped into her. "What?" she whispered.

"I thought I heard something move over there to the right," Verity whispered back. They stood motionless.

"I can't hear anything. The river's too noisy. I don't see anything either."

Verity relaxed. "It's probably an animal."

Violet grabbed her and almost dropped her blanket. "What kind of animal?" she whispered loudly.

Verity shrugged. "Maybe a bear?"

"A bear?!" gasped Violet in horror.

"Shhhh!"

They listened again and after a moment, Verity proceeded toward the river. It wasn't very far from their shelter, but it was a formidable task to keep their balance on rough ground in the dark while trying to be quiet.

At last, they reached the riverbank and squatted down on rocks to wait and watch for fairies. It was pleasantly cool by the water. Gradually, the fireflies flew closer and closer. Verity shrugged off her blanket, lunged, and slipped on the grassy bank. One foot stepped into the cold water. She sat down abruptly on a rock. After a minute of watchful silence, she tried again.

"Got it!" she cried out.

"Shhhhhh!" warned Violet.

"Look, it doesn't look like a bug."

"Make your wish."

"I wish..."

"Don't say it out loud; it must be a secret."

"Done! Now it lights three times. One... two—that's dimmer... three! This wish-granting must make fairies weak."

"That's three—let it go!"

Verity threw open her hands and stood in her night shift watching the firefly escape over the river. She thought she saw something move on the other side of the water but wasn't quite sure.

"Now it's my turn," declared Violet, forgetting to whisper altogether in her excitement.

Verity sat down and pulled her blanket around her. The night air was cooling at last and she shivered, but while Violet jumped around trying to catch her fairy, Verity watched the other bank. It didn't look like a bear. It looked more like a horse!

"Got it," said Violet. "Now, I wish..." she paused, "...and one... two... oh dear, please light again. Oh no! Maybe I killed it... three! There it is. Thank you, dear fairy, I release you!" She spread her arms and the fairy light blinked again as it flew away.

"Hark!"

From the other side of the caravan came a shout. Grabbing blankets, giggling, and grunting, the girls ran in haste across the uneven meadow into their shelter and onto their mats.

"Who's there?" muttered the maid. "Are you alright, Lady Violet?"

"Yes, Griselda, we're fine. Go back to sleep." Soon the other woman was snoring again.

The camp grew quiet.

Then Violet whispered, "I have to pee!"

Verity giggled.

Chapter 22

STORM'S FURY

Long after Violet had settled herself to sleep, Verity lay awake listening to the sounds of the night. The low rumble of a distant storm sounded gentle and almost soothing. It was still muggy and hot, and she wished she could be down by the river where it was cool. She thought of the horse standing pale in the woods on the other side, and wondered where its rider could have been that the creature would just stand there so still.

Violet sighed in her sleep. Verity thought about Violet's wish. It was easy to guess that she asked for a satisfying outcome of their visit to the Marquis and that his son would be handsome and kind. Violet was probably dreaming of him now.

The distant thunder growled again. It could signal a cooler day tomorrow. Verity turned over on her pallet and faced the river. *Could a fairy possibly grant my wish?* she wondered, *knowing she had wished a double wish.* She recalled her thoughts: *I wish to have my loving parents return safe and well, and I wish to find my true love.*

She concentrated on her parents in hope that if she could will that part of her wish to come true, then the rest of her life would smooth itself out. She felt herself drifting toward sleep. Verity imagined she could see her mother's warm brown loving eyes, and that she was trying to speak to her. Her voice was low, and the words were blurred. The sound changed, rumbling like a man's voice. Then she saw the brown eyes of her father. He smiled and spoke.

"I can't hear you," she tried to tell him. He spoke louder, but the words blurred. Then his eyes flashed to a bright blue. He looked distressed. Lighter, he seemed transparent, his hair almost blond. His mouth moved. She tried to understand. A flash of light outlined his small frame, highlighting his fair hair and reflecting in his light blue eyes.

"Father?" she asked, puzzled at the change in him.

And then he answered, "Sunshine!"

A crashing report of thunder woke her up, heart pounding. The storm hung on the hills behind them. The tethered horses whinnied nervously. A flash of lightning lit the scene toward the river. Verity could see a guard climbing up the bank toward the encampment. She sat up abruptly and listened. She could hear the sound of rushing water. The river had been a quiet gurgle before. Now it sounded like a roaring bull.

A sheet of lightning turned night into day. Voices shouted orders. Torches were lit. Verity glimpsed the Duchess fully dressed heading in their direction.

Violet stirred and rose onto her elbow. "Verity? What's happening?" She blinked as another sheet of lightning blinded her sleepy eyes. The clap of thunder drowned out her gasp.

"We'd better get dressed. Your mother is coming. The camp is stirring. Wake Griselda."

Violet shook the maid's shoulder. Griselda woke instantly and was on her feet before Violet. She was an experienced lady's maid and ever alert to the demanding and bad-tempered Duchess.

The Duchess herself leaned into the shelter as a bolt of lightning flashed on the hill. She saw the three stirring and preparing to dress.

"We move at once. Do not delay us!"

Violet's voice trembled. "In the dark, Mother?"

"Darcus knows the way—especially in the black of night. Hurry now. No time to lose. The river is rising. We must cross before it floods or we'll lose several days."

Violet grumbled to herself as she dressed. Fumbling in her haste, she dropped her comb on her pallet. Busy hands collected pallets, blankets, and pillows for packing.

"My comb!" Violet cried. As the servants passed Verity, another sheet of lightning lit the scene. The comb protruded from the folds of bedding. Verity had but an instant flash of the jewelled comb. She snatched at it and pulled. Blinded by the light as dark once more enfolded all, Verity felt with her left hand, grabbed the shoulder of her friend, and swept the comb over and into her chest. Violet's hands caught it and she shoved it into her hair. There was no time for gratitude.

Verity's hand on Violet's shoulder pulled her urgently. "Come! Let us find our palfreys. The grooms will be packing carts. We may have to saddle up ourselves."

They snatched up their panniers and rushed headlong through the dark even as the first cart started down the road.

The grassy meadow where the horses were tethered was a mass of moving men and animals. By the light of a single torch at the side of the road, Verity and Violet held hands to keep their balance as they made their way toward the area where they had left their palfreys. A nervous mare pulled harshly by a groom snorted as they approached. A flash of lightning reflected in the animal's eyes as its neck extended as far as it could go. The poor animal moved sideways in panic. The moving wall of horseflesh staggered toward the girls, but at the last minute gloved hands guided them sideways out of harm's way.

"Your palfreys are ready. Over here—this way."

The two girls went out of the confusion to a small oak beside the road and up onto the saddles with assisting hands. They were led to the torch-lit area where cart followed cart out of the light and down the road with only a distant torch-lit cart to guide them.

For once, Verity was relieved to see the Duke. With calm authority, he directed the melee of his household servants into order. Carts came out of darkness into the circle of light to be directed onto the road. From beyond, back in the campground, came the strident voice of the Duchess whipping sluggish servants into haste. Verity's gaze took in the scene and finally rested on the face of their rescuer, Sir Albertus. With one hand, he held the reins of the two palfreys while with the other he held the bridle of his destrier. The big steed seemed to feed off his calm.

Verity took a deep breath and let it out slowly.

Violet watched her father and also began to calm down. Her chin lifted in pride and, for once, she felt a confidence in her father that she hadn't known was there. She saw him nod to Sir Albertus and then, after a conference with the driver of her cart, he strode quickly over to them.

"You are ready, Berty?"

"Yes, sire!"

"Then be off and cross as soon as you can. The girls are in your care. They are your priority. The Duchess and I will be right behind you. This is Violet's cart. Give orders for it to go across as soon as possible, but stay with the girls. Here comes Brownie to drive. Hie, Brownie! Up you go!" The little man gave a jump onto the back of Violet's cart.

Sir Albertus carefully handed each of the girls the reins of their horses. He mounted his destrier, and as the cart squeaked its way onto the road, Violet's palfrey followed. He slapped Verity's palfrey on the rump and the three of them joined the caravan. The cart just ahead held a torch, which guided them in the dark.

A breeze fluttered the leaves and carried the Duchess's strident voice.

"I'll teach you. When I say move, I mean now!"

A scream split the night and a lightning flash was followed by a harsh crack. The storm was closing in on them fast.

"Is it far to the crossing?" ventured Verity.

Sir Albertus rubbed his chin with his gloved knuckle. "Not far, but we'll be wet before we get there—cover up," he replied.

Lightning clearly showed the expression on his face and Verity guessed that they were in for a rough time. The girls pulled up their hoods and closed their cloaks just as, with a furious gust of wind, the rain began to pelt down on the struggling caravan. The rain beat upon them in sheets driven by the wind. Before long, the girls were soaked. There was no relief from the pelting rain and plodding pace. The Duke and Duchess passed the caravan on the side of the trail.

"You're almost there. Stay in line. The side trail is uneven. We'll go ahead," the Duke breathlessly shouted over the sound of the rain. The Duke and Duchess pulled ahead and were gone.

It seemed to Verity that it took the rest of the night to arrive where they would ford the river, but it was still black as pitch except for a few spitting torches under the trees. From her viewpoint, Verity could see four carts already in the water with horses frightened and struggling, doing their best to pull across to the far shore. One horse twisted his neck as he stumbled in the water and his eyes bulged with terror. Verity reached and patted Dolphus on his neck and he shivered in response. The clearing was jammed with carts and they had to wait. The river level was rising rapidly. What had been a gurgling shallow expanse was now halfway up the wheels of the carts.

"Send them two at a time!" ordered the Duchess.

The Duke's voice rose, "It can't be done. The crossing is too narrow for two carts. One would be pushed into deep water."

"We will lose our opportunity to cross," countered the Duchess. "Send two before it gets too deep."

As one horse entered the water, the Duchess's whip sailed through the air and, with a scream of fright, the second horse bolted into the froth next to it. The two horses struggled gradually to the midpoint. The driver of the right-hand cart pulled his best to keep his horse leaning upstream and away from the second cart. But gradually, as if he shied, his horse pressed further left. The water rose in a wave near the midpoint. If they could pass that point, they might make it. The two horses pulled and struggled against the power of the water. Gradually, they were pushed downstream, closer to the edge of the deeper part of the riverbed.

There was a murmur from the crowd as a swell in the river crested in the centre, hitting the first cart broadside. The wheels skidded on the bedrock and crashed into the other cart. The second cart's wheels slipped off the edge. Cart, horse, and driver were dumped into deep water and swept away. A few gasps and then silence covered the crowd in dismay. They watched the floating body of the driver bob and crash against rocks as it raced furiously out of sight in the darkness. The cart and horse were upside down as the cart crashed to pieces on the rocks. They, too, disappeared.

"It was only a food cart—move on!" snapped the Duchess and she cracked her whip once more to start the next cart, as the first cart pulled up on the far bank.

This time, the Duchess waited until one cart was ahead before urging on the next with her cracking fury.

The Duke shouted at Darcus, "Keep them moving!" and then at Albertus, "Bring my daughter next."

Then he turned and slapped the Duchess's horse. Pulling on her reins, he forced her into the water. The Duchess was too busy controlling her horse in the rushing water to protest, and soon found herself on the opposite bank, powerless to bully the caravan. The rain continued its downpour. Darcus kept up the pressure to move the carts. The bottleneck at the water's edge seemed impossible for Albertus and his young charges to get through.

Albertus swore as he attempted to manoeuvre their horses closer. At last, he leapt from his destrier, pulled Darcus off his saddle, and dumped him in a bush. While Darcus yelled in outrage, Albertus grabbed the reins of all three horses and drew them in front of the offending cart. Mounting his horse, Albertus tucked his own reins under his leg and, with the palfreys' reins in each hand, pulled them after him into the water.

"Hang on!" he cried as they neared the centre. Violet and Verity leaned over and put their arms around their horses' necks and hung on. The palfreys, urged on by Albertus, pulled up on either side of the destrier. A surge of water roared down the river. The wave hit Violet and her palfrey first, and Fergus shied into the mighty destrier. The steed did not flinch but his feet slipped sideways on the stone riverbed and his massive rump bumped Verity's palfrey on his front quarters. Dolphus lost his footing and fell, yanking his reins out of Albertus's hand. Verity and Dolphus tumbled sideways into the deep water.

By the silhouette cast from torches on the far shore, the crowd on the bank watched in horror as horse and rider were swept downstream into the dark and out of sight. No one screamed. Verity rose to the tumbling water's surface, feeling its power moving her away from meagre light into darkness. She could hear Dolphus scream behind her. She kicked as well as she could with her skirts and cloak hindering her legs. She pushed and pulled herself in the cold water away from her horse. A jolt against a boulder hurt her shoulder and bounced her further downstream.

The water seemed very deep. She could not feel the riverbed with her feet, so she thought she was above most of the treacherous rocks. Dolphus was quiet. Perhaps he'd drowned. Verity felt a cry swelling in her chest and her face puckered, but then another wave dunked her. She kicked and came up again, sputtering. There was no time to cry if she was going to survive this cold sweep into hell. She continued to kick and she kept her arms out to protect herself.

She had a sense that a cliff edged the river on the right. She was quite close to it, but could not grasp anything. A whinny to her left gave her hope. Dolphus! She called and was dunked again. She kicked, but it was more difficult. She was tiring fast. The rain let up. She pushed her hair out of her eyes. Distant lightning lit the scene. There were cliffs on both sides, but no rocks broke the surface.

It was quieter. Something was coming closer. She could see it sticking out of the water and coming toward her. She was moving fast with the current. She kept kicking, but the shape grew larger. Just as she was going to dodge it, she realized it was Dolphus. She reached out as he swept by her and grabbed the reins. She was yanked through the water and nearly dunked again, but she held on, gradually pulling herself closer to her palfrey. She pulled herself over his back and grabbed his mane. She could feel his body. He was swimming! She thought, *Oh, my friend Dolphus, get me out of here.* She laid her head against his dear sweet horsey neck and passed out.

Chapter 23

AWAKENING

She was cold at the bottom of the hole. Murmuring sounds echoed and swirled around her making her dizzy. She drifted. She felt frightened and confused. Was she drowning? Was this death? Something warm touched her hand. Something soft tickled her face. A murmur sounded close, but she could not understand the words. She drifted in darkness. Warmth roused her. Perhaps she could rise up from this pit of dark. Something warm and soft covered her. Her feet were being massaged. Mmmm! It felt good. No one had ever rubbed her feet except her mother when she was very little.

"Mmm…" She tried to say "Mother" but drifted again.

The murmur roused her once more. Her feet were warm and someone was rubbing her hands. She smelled wood smoke. It irritated her nose and throat, and she sneezed. Her mind began to work.

"Dolphus?" she tried to call and opened her eyes. She looked into intense blue eyes close to her face.

"God bless thee, Fairy Princess," said the smiling face, "you are alive and among the living. Now, wiggle your toes!" He lifted the blanket. Verity dutifully wiggled her toes. He laughed in delight. "Praise God!" he grinned.

Verity had never seen a grin so infectious. She grinned back.

"Now wiggle your fingers."

Verity complied.

He looked so pleased one might have thought he had been given a sweetmeat fancy. "Good!" declared the smiling face and he retreated to his campfire.

Dolphus nickered and limped over to her. Verity lay on the

ground on some bedding and looked up at her palfrey with relief. Beyond him, high on the branch of an oak tree, she thought she saw Rothko. The raven's beady eyes watched her with grave interest. She smiled to think that the Wizard still kept an eye on her, even if it wasn't his own.

"Are you feeling better, Fairy Princess?"

Verity nodded.

The young man offered her a steaming cup of broth. "Easy, slow... just a sip..." he coached as he held her head up.

Verity studied the young man's face as she sipped. Her eyes travelled down the straight nose to his mouth, curved up in a smile. His strong jaw sprouted fine stubble. Light hair tumbled over the side of his face as he tipped his head to study her face as well.

Verity finished the broth. "Who are you?" she ventured.

"A friend," he answered with enough conviction to reassure her.

They looked at each other contentedly, knowing that that was all that mattered.

Verity's eyes grew heavy and she once again drifted off to sleep. This time, she was warm and there was no dark hole.

Verity woke, suddenly full of apprehension. She could still feel the warmth of the blanket and smell the wood fire. Her travelling dress and cloak hung from small branches nearby. Her panniers hung on another. The raven was not in the oak tree. She looked for Dolphus. There he was, to her left, munching on tall grass and buttercups. Not far from her dear palfrey was the young man, drawing his bow and aiming his arrow straight at Dolphus.

Verity screamed, "Nooooo!"

Dolphus bolted for the woods. The young man lowered his bow and shook his head. He walked back to Verity, who rose quickly in shock and alarm. Trembling in distress, she started to sob. He dropped the bow and took her into his arms.

"It's all right," he soothed, stroking her hair and patting her back. "I didn't shoot your horse."

Verity pulled back. "Why? Why were you going to kill my Dolphus?" she sobbed.

He held her hand. "I'm sorry, little Fairy Princess, but I think he has a broken leg. He's limping badly and I didn't want him to suffer. I cannot bear to see animals in pain."

Verity shook her head. "No, no, no! You don't understand. Dolphus was injured when he was very young. He always limps when he's tired, but it passes. His leg isn't broken! Don't shoot him!" Her voice rose to a screech and she cried again.

"Don't cry. Please don't cry!" He held her close and rocked her gently. "I promise I won't shoot your palfrey. I promise!"

Verity slowly controlled herself. There was one after-quake to her sobbing and then she was still. His arms tightened when she shivered. She liked that. Slowly, she raised her head from his shoulder, soaked with her tears. He partly released her and searched her face. Her steady gaze told him all he wanted to know. He kissed her gently on the mouth, then, holding her tightly, he kissed her with all the feelings that dwelled inside his soul. Verity tingled in unexpected parts of her body. She held on tightly and wished he would never stop, but then, gently, he let her go. She smiled at him, shyly.

"I'm not a Fairy Princess, kind sir," Verity said, trying to think of something to say.

"You are to me!" he said vehemently.

Verity's eyes widened as she sensed the strength of his feelings. She knew she was a worthy person because she would not willingly hurt another, but she needed to know something more—something that was important to her.

"Do I not look like a frog?" she asked abruptly.

He looked at her dumbfounded, but the serious expression on her face warned him not to laugh. His chest was almost bursting with joy, but he dare not laugh.

He said simply, "No. You are truly a beautiful Fairy Princess."

Verity took his face in her hands and kissed him until she heard the sound of trumpets. She threw her arms around his neck and kissed him again. Blaring trumpets sounded closer. She released him suddenly.

"What is that?"

He blinked. Dizzy and wanting more, he kept his arms around her and answered hoarsely, "My hunting party, I fear. We were separated yesterday. They're probably looking for me."

Verity looked down at her chemise. She blushed. "I am not dressed. Please give me my clothes."

He smiled and reached up for her gown and cloak. Hastily, Verity pulled on hose and boots, and threw her gown overhead. She snatched her girdle and cloak with no notice of his amusement or the beginning of panic in his eyes.

"Please, sir. Where is Castle Cortelaide? I understand it is close to this river."

"About an hour's ride toward the setting sun on this side of the river, but there's no hurry. My party is coming. We are going that way. We will escort you."

Verity whistled shrilly. Dolphus whinnied and trotted out of the woods. She spotted Rothko circling overhead.

"There is no need of an escort, sir. I have an escort of a different kind. Thank you for your kindness. I shall never forget you."

She kissed him again and, with a jump worthy of a knight, she was astride her palfrey and on her way.

Taken by surprise by her sudden speed, he ran after her. "Wait! Where will I find you? What is your name?"

Verity was already disappearing into the forest scrub.

He turned back and ran for his white steed just as his hunting party arrived in triumph for having found their Prince. They would have forfeited their lives if they had lost the King's son on a simple hunting trip. The men were so pleased with themselves they did not notice the Prince retrieving the tiny pink rose made of ribbon that had fallen from the Fairy Princess's glade-green gown. He hastily tucked it into his doublet and assured himself that he at least knew her destination.

Chapter 24

IN DISGUISE

Verity urged Dolphus on to greater speed. She could hear the hounds and shouts of the men behind her, but she was fairly certain they had not seen her departure. Her green clothes blended with the green forest, which was fairly dense. She looked up to see Rothko circling ahead of her. She was confident he would lead her directly to Violet.

Branches lightly pulled at her clothes and hair. She suddenly thought of her appearance. She hadn't combed her hair since yesterday. She probably looked like a drowned cat or an untidy frog. No! She pulled Dolphus to a halt. She grimly reprimanded herself. "I do not look like a frog. That wicked harridan is making me think that I am a frog by innuendo and suggestion." With a smug grimace, she added, "Won't Duchess Euphoria be surprised when I show up like a ghost on the doorstep!"

Verity dismounted and pulled her girdle, cloak, and pannier down from Dolphus's back. She walked to the river. The flash flood had subsided, leaving pools of still water beyond the river's edge. Verity looked down at her watery reflection. Backlit by the sun, a creature with pale hair tumbling frothily around its face stared back at her.

Have I gone grey overnight? she wondered and held up a thick strand of her long hair to inspect. She was shocked to see it was very fair—almost blonde. She sat there by the river combing the snarls from her hair slowly and thoughtfully. Could river water lighten hair? She thought not. Dolphus was the same dear colour he'd always been and her travelling gown was still a deep green. Logically, she realized she must be a blonde, and then she thought about her own special soap that her mother insisted was necessary. Why was it necessary? It changed her hair from blonde to mousy brown. Her mother's hair was deep brunette and her father's was dark, too. They both had dark brown eyes. Hers were blue.

Verity was suddenly chilled. *Who am I?* Her whole world tilted and she felt like a stranger examining herself. Again, she looked in the mirror of the water and down at the body she'd always thought familiar. She looked down her bodice and was jolted by the appearance of her breasts. She was a small person and her breasts were small, but she realized they were developed. She thought of Violet—bigger, sturdier, but definitely still flat. *I could be older than Violet. Am I disguised? Why would I be disguised?*

Remembering the gentle young man and the feelings she felt when they kissed, Verity resolved to find out the answers. She couldn't live her life in limbo. She must know! Shaking off her reverie, she glanced at the midday sun. She must catch up to Violet.

Then another glance in the small pool sent her digging in her panniers. She carried her special soap in this travel bag. Would it be still usable after its exposure to river water? She got it out and carefully unwrapped it. A little water had made it rather soggy, but it was all right. As quickly as she could, she washed her hair in the river using lots of soap. She dried her hair with her cloak, combed it once more, and braided the brown mousy hair into plaits. Tidying her clothes and donning her girdle and damp cloak, she mounted Dolphus and looked up. There ahead sat the raven on a tree branch, patiently waiting. She waved and he flew ahead once more, leading her on.

"Thank you, dear Wizard, for your guidance and protection, but you are going to have to answer questions when I return." She considered her situation as she determinedly urged Dolphus in the direction of the soaring black bird.

When Verity finally emerged from the dense woods, she found the road leading west. From then on, she made good time. She let Dolphus run at a full gallop, and grinned to herself as she thought of his lame leg, *Lame indeed! Not my Dolphus! That bad habit of yours almost cost you your life, my dear beast!* Dolphus whinnied at the sheer joy of their wild ride.

Soon they passed through areas with cottages, pastures, and cultivated fields. Dolphus slowed as the ground rose to a hill. Verity reined him in at the summit for a rest as she studied the magnificent vista of the Castle de Cortelaide—her destination. Dusty pink puffs rose from the road leading to the castle. A slowly moving large entourage was approaching the gate—Violet!

Verity patted Dolphus and whispered, "Oats, my friend! I shall see that you have the best. We have caught up to Violet before they made the castle. Think oats, Dolphus. Let's go!" and she tapped him on his rump. Dolphus didn't need a second hint. He galloped down the hill at top speed. The sound of his galloping drew the weary travellers' attention. Heads turned and people gasped when they saw the small figure clad in green.

"It's Mistress Verity!" called Griselda from her seat on the Duchess's cart. "Thanks to God and his mercy!"

Violet heard the shouts behind her. *Not more trouble,* she thought listlessly. Her face was blotchy and her eyes were swollen from crying. Her hair was tied untidily like a horse's tail and hung limply to the side of her face. Another shout sounded, nearer this time, and she heard not distressing fear, but joy. She turned to look and there was Dolphus with Verity riding full-speed with her dark green cloak billowing out behind.

Violet uttered a guttural moan and slid off her moving palfrey. She was running before her feet touched the ground.

Verity pulled hard on Dolphus, who reared at the unexpected signal. He snorted in disappointment. Verity let go, dismounted like a feather, and ran to Violet. The two girls held each other like a vow.

"I thought you were dead," sobbed Violet.

"I know, I know!" whispered Verity, "but I'm here."

"Zocks! What do you know!" came the cold sarcastic voice of the Duchess. "The frog floats! But of course, frogs love water, do they not?" She turned her back to the girls and continued on to the castle gates.

Chapter 25

A MOTHER'S TOUCH

At Violet's request, Verity was billeted in her room in Castle Cortelaide. They talked until they fell asleep exhausted, but Verity never mentioned the handsome young man. Nor did she say a word about her blonde hair. She needed answers, but she must be careful of whom she asked the questions. She was spared embarrassing omissions and awkward pauses in the relating of her story, as Violet purged herself of the horrors of losing Verity, quarrelling parents, cart repairs, and animal injuries. Once relieved, Violet dwelled on hopes for the morrow when she would meet Lucien, the son of the Marquis.

Exhausted, Violet fell asleep and in the ember-lit quiet of the room, and Verity's thoughts drifted back to the young man's smile, his tickling fair hair, his blue eyes, and his muscular arms... She smiled as she drifted and, at last, slept.

The smell of wood smoke curled through Verity's dreams. She smiled as she felt the tickle of hair against her cheek. The young man was there, rubbing her hands and smiling. She felt as if she were falling into the blue pools of his eyes. His words were the same, "Awaken, awaken."

...but the voice was a woman's. "Awaken! Awaken, my darling beauties. The water won't stay hot all morning. Travelling is such a dusty business, isn't it? Oh, to be young and have such roses for cheeks. Oh my dears, I've always wanted a daughter. Perhaps I'll have my wish! And today, I have two!"

Violet and Verity sat up in the huge poster bed and stared at the servants setting up two tubs and filling them with hot water. Such luxury. A bath in one's chamber? They couldn't believe it, and the little woman who was accomplishing this task was dressed in golden brocade. She was a chubby sight to behold—a golden orb that practically rolled around the room for her round body was never still. Her hands flew, directing her servants. Occasionally, she grabbed a shoulder, turning a young girl toward the door, and playfully spanking her to keep her moving. The manoeuvre seemed to be necessary because the young girls, who were toting pails of steaming water to the tubs, were inclined to pause and gape at the two young ladies in the bed.

Violet started to titter. Verity grinned from ear to ear. At first it seemed that there was an army of girls, but then it became apparent that the same girls were making multiple trips. Verity found it easy to identify the first girl as she made her second trip around with a bucket. She wore a red kerchief and red apron of the finest brocade. It could have been made from scraps from Milady's worn-out clothes. So the woman, hard though it might be to believe, must be the Marquise herself. Surely a servant could not wear such clothes?

The Lady turned, beaming, and approached the bed on Violet's side. She lifted the young face with a bejewelled hand.

"Surely you must be Violet! Fair complexion, ebony hair, such beauty, and those violet eyes! Lucien will be smitten instantly." She patted Violet's cheek. "You look like your mother. And you..." she looked at Verity. "A fairy elf with your blue eyes so sparkling! You do not look like the Duchess at all. But you're still adorable! Now, I wonder if my nephew...?" Finger poised on chin, she paused.

"We're not sisters, you understand, Milady... ah..." began Violet.

"Doesn't matter, doesn't matter. Oh! I forgot to say that the Duchess has already bathed and there isn't much time before the water cools." She gestured, "This is Fiametta." Fiametta, with the red apron and kerchief, bowed, giggling.

"She will help you with your bath. The drying cloths are there and there is plenty of soap. If you hurry, you will have time to stroll in the rose garden before I see you at dinner in the Great Hall.

Oh! I almost forgot! Here, I awakened you after your harrowing journey and neglected to introduce myself. I am the Marquise Isabella de Cortelaide, your happy hostess. My husband, Arthur, is so looking forward to meeting you. Oh! I forgot! Pagley has your breakfast." She indicated a short girl by the window table. "Enjoy yourselves!" And she left the room.

The childlike Pagley gave a small curtsy and curls bobbed around her face while she struggled to keep from laughing.

"I think I'm going to like it here," announced Violet as she jumped down from the bed, helped herself to the honey buns on the tray, and lifted a tankard of mulled wine. "What hospitality! Is the Marquise always so jolly?" she asked Pagley.

Pagley giggled like a bubbling brook and Fiametta answered, "The Marquise Isabella is a dear... sweet, generous, warm-hearted..."

"Saint!" finished Pagley, who had finally stopped giggling, and looked so solemn that Violet and Verity stopped eating and stared at her. Pagley stared back for a moment before she turned and limped jerkily over to the window.

Fiametta whispered, "Milady Isabella saved Pagley's life when she was crushed by a wagon wheel. She was only three years old and after she revived, they said she'd never walk, but..."

"Enough!" said Pagley sharply. "The water will be cold if you let Fiametta keep talking."

Violet and Verity dutifully followed directives from Fiametta and gradually realized that Pagley was in charge: Fiametta followed her every suggestion as though they were from the Marquise herself.

Verity whispered to Fiametta, "How old is the child, Pagley?"

Fiametta grinned broadly as she scrubbed Violet's back. "She is no child. She has been with Milady for nineteen years!"

Fiametta sobered then and said, "It's easy to misunderstand because she looks so short, but terrible things happened to her legs and feet. She is an amazing miracle and we're all fond of her."

"Hurry! Time to dry!" announced Pagley, holding out drying

cloths for the girls. "Your clothes chests are here. Fia will help you dress. Later!" she picked up the tray and scurried out of the room in her bumpy fashion.

Chapter 26

A MISS IN THE MAZE

The garden was superb. The roses smelled sweet and fresh from the morning dew, and there was a path that invited the girls to wander.

"Look at the size of the yellow ones!" exclaimed Verity.

"And those white roses have a beautiful pink blush!" answered Violet.

A gardener was busy weeding. Verity complimented him on the roses. He smiled, showing big teeth.

Verity asked, "How do you make the flowers grow so large?"

He shrugged and uttered rapidly in a foreign tongue.

Verity shook her head in puzzlement.

He smiled, pointed to the castle and said "Da kazza!"

He bounced around the garden gesturing, until Violet laughed and said, "He means the Marquise. What a perfect imitation! She is a remarkable woman. Look at the red roses. Have you ever seen any colour so brilliant?"

Verity turned to look and suddenly remembered the dark red flowers of the swamp. As she shuddered at the memory, the Duchess appeared from behind a hedge. "You don't like red flowers, dear Toadie?"

Verity shrank from the tall Duchess and hid her face so Euphoria couldn't see her distaste. She curtsied for good measure to keep the Duchess from seeing how much she disliked her and said, "No Milady, I prefer pink flowers."

"Of course!" murmured the Duchess, "The pink flowers on the lily pads," and she gestured beyond Verity.

Verity turned to see a lovely pond covered with pink lilies. A frog jumped from a pad into the water with a *kerplunk*.

"Come to visit your relatives, dear Verity?" laughed the Duchess. "Just a little nudge from me and you could have a refreshing dip. You seem to enjoy the water... ha, ha, ha!"

Verity hurried down the path away from the dreadful woman and her torments. She had turned a few corners before she was aware that she had entered a maze. She hoped she wouldn't get lost. At once it was quiet. Shrubs towered around her small frame. She could hear Violet's laughter in the distance and the muted voice of a young man. Again Violet laughed.

Verity continued to walk the path through the hedges. She hoped the Duchess wouldn't appear around the next corner. She kept walking. The sun was getting high. It would soon be time for dinner in the Great Hall. A horse nickered beyond the hedge. Then she heard a voice and stopped. She knew the sound of that voice; she would never forget it. He was coming closer. She listened intently.

He said, "Yes, fair of face, with golden hair and blue eyes. She asked for this castle, but..." The horse whinnied and drowned out his voice. "Steady, old fellow!"

His voice sounded higher. Verity looked to the top of the hedge, but it was too high even were he mounted on the horse. She couldn't see him.

"I'm here!" she called, but her throat was so dry after the fright she'd had from the Duchess that she croaked the words. She cleared her throat.

"Never mind, old friend. I'll find her somehow. Thank you."

A deeper voice called, "Good luck!" as the sound of departing hooves defeated any hope of being heard.

Verity tore a leaf from the shrubbery and ripped it to tiny pieces in her frustration.

"Don't be silly," she chided herself. "Why would he be looking for you?"

Violet exclaimed, "There she is! Verity! This is Lucien!"

Verity liked young Lucien on sight. He was tall, with straight dark hair that seemed a bit unruly. A cowlick sprouted from the crown of his head. Dark eyebrows moved with his laughing eyes. She smiled at him as she thought, *He's perfect for Violet—they are a pair.*

Lucien took her hand and brushed his lips over it. "Lady Verity! My sincere apology for interrupting your garden stroll, but it is time to gather in the Great Hall." He offered his arms to the girls and, three abreast, they walked toward the castle spires that were visible above the greenery. Verity felt confidence emanate from Lucien and she began to feel hope.

ℭhapter 27

HEAR YE! HEAR YE!

Feasting in Cortelaide Castle was a boisterous affair, and Verity and Violet were enjoying every noisy bit of it. Contrary to the supposed rumours of animosity toward the Duchess, Arthur—the Marquis de Cortelaide—was catering to every whim the demanding Duchess could invent. He did so not only with wit and charm, but he also added a generous dollop of flattery. The Duchess looked as though she was at last being appreciated and the occasional smile relaxed her otherwise icy beauty.

The Marquise had no problem with the Duke either. She laced her deferring attentiveness with humour and the occasional blatant but sincere admiration of his daughter, so he also was charmed.

Lucien managed to look after both girls during the meal while telling amusing stories. Verity thought him a born storyteller. Lucien had just returned from a hunting trip. It seemed every one of his hunting party had fouled up in an alarming fashion and ended in either dire humiliation or total triumph.

"Our losing the Prince was a roustabout. Can you imagine? We even searched the swamp. That was where Simon almost lost his mount in the sucking mud..."

Verity didn't want to know about swamps. The memory of the hideous and evil flowers haunted her, and she shut off her attention to Lucien and focused on her food and the juggler who sang as he entertained their table. She concentrated on his song and didn't hear a word Lucien spoke until the juggler stopped singing. The juggler then moved away from their table and Verity tasted the plum pudding that Lucien had put on her trencher.

Lucien was saying to Violet, "Can you believe it? He tried to shoot the horse!"

Verity froze. Lucien had to be talking about the young man from the woods. *He must know who the young man is,* she thought. *Why didn't I ask? Why was he here today?* She looked around the room quickly. He wasn't in the room, but Lucien must know him.

She turned to Lucien. He was laughing with Violet, "But that wasn't the best part. When he fell off the cart, he landed headfirst in the cook's soup." Violet was laughing so much that she hadn't touched her plum pudding, which was a favourite of hers.

Verity touched Lucien on his arm.

"Who was the young man?"

"His name's Si-Si-Simon," stuttered Lucien. "He is a real klutz!"

"And is he fair?" asked Verity.

"Oh, always," replied Lucien. "He would never cheat a living soul!"

"I mean is his colouring fair?" persisted Verity.

Lucien looked puzzled, and then he pointed to the table before them. "Down there at the end, the fellow with the black curly hair, that's Simon."

"Oh. Thank you," replied Verity and returned to finish her plum pudding. Embarrassed, she thought Lucien would think ill of her for being too forward. But Lucien just returned to amusing Violet and quickly forgot Verity's question.

Negotiations for a merger of the two families proceeded slowly. From what she could observe, Verity realized that the Marquise was taking her time to be sure that the young couple were becoming friends, while on the other side, the Duchess was trying to make a deal that would favour herself economically. Any animosity toward the Duke and Duchess of Grenwoodle was well hidden by the Cortelaides.

Their party had been guests at the castle about a week when it became apparent that the Grenwoodles and the Cortelaides had almost secured a deal. It was also obvious that Violet and Lucien were in love. Everyone gathered for dinner in the Great Hall, buzzing in anticipation of an announcement. Indeed, the crowd was poised ready to clap or cheer at the good news when a messenger was announced and given the floor.

From a scroll he read, "Hear ye! Hear ye! His majesty announces that his son Prince Nicholas will travel throughout the land searching for his bride. Hear ye! Hear ye! Be prepared and rejoice to receive your next King. Present all eligible maidens to his Royal Highness and be ready to celebrate!"

There followed an itinerary of the Prince's expected travels. The Duchess stood immediately after the messenger had completed his duty.

"We pack at once," she announced. "We must be home to entertain the Prince," and she walked out.

Violet and Lucien looked at each other in utter dismay. Verity looked at the Duke. He stared in shock at his wife's retreating figure. The Marquise plucked at his velvet sleeve.

"Do something!" she pleaded. "Stop your wife! Think of your daughter's happiness!"

The Duke rose without a word and followed the Duchess. His face completely lacked expression.

Lucien held Violet in his arms. Tears ran down her cheeks, and his face, usually so jovial, was as grim as his father's. He looked over to his father whose eyes met his and a look of understanding passed between them. Verity observed the exchange of thought between father and son, and watched the Marquise stand and put her arms around her husband's neck as she watched Violet silently weep. The room was abuzz with shock and disappointment.

Verity stood and pulled Violet to her feet. "Come, dear friend, come. We have to go."

Violet whispered, "How can she be so cruel? I am her daughter! I'll never forgive her for this."

Verity stroked her dark hair and looked past her friend to Lucien. "It will all work out well. I promise, Violet. Be patient, dear friend. We must go home now, but everything will be fine."

The two girls walked slowly through the Hall. "How could she? She has ruined it all," cried Violet.

Verity's small figure supported her friend. At the door, Violet turned and looked back at Lucien. Their eyes met. Then with a sob, Violet ran down the passageway. Verity noted that among the hushed crowd there wasn't one face without tears. She nodded to Lucien, who stood with his hand on his mother's shoulder. The Marquis had not even risen with respect at his guests' departure. His dark grey unruly hair looked like a thundercloud. His eyes emitted lightning rage. Together, the three—Lucien and his parents—looked solidly formidable. Verity nodded at them and turned away with a certain confidence in her own brave words.

Chapter 28

OL' AGGIE KNOWS

The journey home was much shorter; not having to stop at the Baron's Castle, they followed a more direct route. Verity was relieved to lie on her own bed in the Garret. This was the first time in weeks that she was alone and could think without disruption.

She couldn't blame Violet for crying. She felt overwhelmed herself. A tear rolled down her cheek, but she brushed it away angrily. There was no time for self-pity when Violet needed a strong friend. She concentrated on Violet.

A few weeks ago, Violet would have been so excited to be in this position. As a noble maiden of marriageable age—beautiful, graceful, intelligent—she now would have two most agreeable possibilities: the Prince and the young nobleman Lucien. It was plain that Lucien was smitten and inconceivable that the Prince would be disinterested in such a lovely young maiden, so the only factors at odds were Violet's obvious feelings for Lucien (she loved him) and the Duchess's feelings for powerful wealth (she loved wealth even more than she loved her own daughter). Euphoria was more than selfish and ruthless. She was wicked. She had no redeeming qualities. She had a formidable power and an evil soul. What a combination.

Verity shuddered. She climbed out of bed, knelt on the floor, and prayed. Then she returned to her bed and hoped that God would inspire her so that she could help Violet. Having called on God for help, Verity felt more peaceful and relaxed. She began to think of the handsome hunter. Visualizing his steady blue eyes made her feel much safer and her memory of the expression in them made her feel worthy and even desirable. She smiled and then dozed.

With startling suddenness, she sat up, wide awake. Inspiration had entered her with total clarity. The Duchess Euphoria was not entirely powerful. She had a weakness—her drugging swamp flowers. But if those flowers could be destroyed... And Verity realized she was not alone. She had an ally—the Wizard. He could tell her how to destroy those wicked plants. She must determine the timing, which would be crucial. Luckily, the Duchess would be preoccupied with preparations for the Prince's arrival and would never notice the activities or spying by "an insignificant toad."

The days slipped by as Verity observed the Duchess's behaviour. There were times when the woman was elated, energetic, and pleasantly cheerful. During this stage, she would treat servants kindly, though always disdainfully. Then would follow a slump. For no apparent reason, she would be highly irritable and demanding. During this time, everyone strove to make no mistakes, for she was quick to dissolve into rages, inflicting damage on any unfortunate bystander. Most of the time, the Duke was absent from the castle, but when he appeared he looked despondent and haunted.

Once, Verity, who was hurrying to run an unnecessary errand for the Duchess, was surprised to see the Duke with his arms around his weeping daughter. His face was a mirror of despair. In a flash of insight, Verity thought, *If the man had any power he wouldn't give in to despair; he would fight for his child.* The thought put a further burden on her shoulders, but she wasn't ready to give up. She hadn't yet consulted the Wizard.

One day, while on yet another task, she talked to old Agatha in the Scullery. Every wrinkle on the old woman's face seemed to smile at the young girl she loved most in the world. She hugged Verity tightly. She whispered, "I'm so glad you didn't drown, dear child!" Then she pushed her away. "You've grown!" she exclaimed in wonder.

Verity laughed. "Agatha, you say that every time. Now I know you're teasing me. See my gown still covers my ankles." She demonstrated.

Agatha's face still held amused astonishment, "No dear girl, you've grown—out!" She demonstrated with a hand gesture from her own bosom. "And," she looked closely into Verity's eyes and waggled a finger at her, "you've met him!"

Verity blushed, looking down, then up in wide-eyed innocence. "What are you talking about, old thing, I've met a great many people. I've just travelled!" She flounced around the Scullery in demonstration to distract Agatha from her probing questions. "And such nice people, too. Oh, dear Agatha, you would love the Marquise. She is a fine lady and a wonderful mother. She pampered Violet and me so extravagantly. We even had baths in our bedchamber—two separate baths with fresh hot water for each of us! She is just magnificent. She would do anything for her husband and Lucien…"

"So! Now you admit there is a he—who is he?" smirked the old woman. She had won the skirmish and looked like a fat old cat that had just tasted fresh cream.

Verity looked steadily at her old friend. "Please don't say anything. I have not said a word to anyone and you are just guessing." The old woman shook her head in denial. Verity continued slowly. "I did meet a nice hunter who rescued me from the cold of the river. He was very kind, but I don't know his name and I'll never see him again."

"He put a light in your eyes, Missy. Old Agatha knows."

"Well, he was handsome and so kind and… he kissed me." Verity blushed.

"Ahhhh… I see," said Agatha.

"Yes, well… I've never been kissed, so perhaps that's it."

"Mmm," said Agatha. They stood in understanding silence. Then Agatha roused, "I have news!" Agatha always heard the gossip first. "The old Baron died."

"The Baron?"

"You know, the old broken-down fox who wanted to marry Lady Violet!"

"Agatha, how do you hear these fantasies of gossip?"

Agatha's wrinkles arranged themselves in smug lines and cagily she added, "The old fart gave himself heart failure trying to put out a fire, I heard."

Verity was dumbstruck. "The poor thing," she mumbled.

Agatha raised an eyebrow. "That's not all, little bird. His son returned with a wifey and lots of money, so I heard."

"I hope he'll do well. I wish him the best. The Duchess did not treat his father kindly."

Agatha kept a beady eye on Verity. "I expect you'll be hearing from them soon."

"Perhaps we will, old dear. Good to see you again. I mustn't keep the Duchess waiting." Briskly, Verity turned away to continue with her tasks. "Oh! I forgot!" Verity giggled at her own unconscious mimicry of the Marquise. "I wish to speak to the Wizard. Could that be arranged? I could probably go to his cottage if I could manage it so the Duchess wouldn't miss me!"

"Not now, Dearie, the old ghost and his black-feathered friend have gone to visit the new Baron and Baroness. He'll be gone a while, but old Aggie will let you know when he returns."

"Oh, thank you, Agatha. I shall wait to hear from you," said Verity as she left.

Agatha grinned at Verity's retreating back. "You'll hear from them, too, I betcha!" and she giggled until her crooked teeth showed.

Chapter 29

INVITATIONS TO THE BALL

Plans for the Ball in the Prince's honour were developing. As the Duke fretted over every gold coin to be spent, the Duchess airily overrode his whimpering complaints and added to the guest list. She was determined that every noble in the area would witness her greatest triumph when she married her daughter to the future king.

The tournament was planned first. It would begin the festivities. The many guests needed accommodation and would have to be entertained and fed sumptuously. The Duchess drove everyone to make the preparations she demanded. Of course, new gowns were needed for the Ball. The draper came with dozens of rolls of fabric, and she contemplated them tirelessly. At last, she ordered a dazzling bright violet cloth for her daughter and a deep, almost black purple for herself. She ordered pale yellow-gold for the rest of the household who would attend.

Violet was enthusiastic about the choice of yellow for her friend. "It will be so refreshing to see you dressed in a new colour, Verity. A golden yellow will set off your brown hair and blue eyes. Perhaps the Prince will be smitten with you and it will all work out as you predicted."

Hope kindled a gleam in her eye "…and then Lucien and I…" she faltered, "…could marry and live happily ever after." Tears glistened in her violet eyes.

Verity gave her friend a hug and looked out at the patch of blue sky through the window. She wished Rothko would come and signal the return of the Wizard. Only one small white cloud drifted past her view.

"Everything will be fine," she reassured her friend and herself.

One day the Duchess learned that the Baron's son had returned. She was reviewing her guest list in the Salon.

"The old skinflint must have died," she remarked callously to her husband. "I wonder if the son is worthy of our favour. At least it cannot disrupt our celebration to have one more—correction—two more to observe our triumph. The news is that he is married, but childless. Perfect. We shall invite them to our Ball. See to it," she ordered her husband.

Verity observed this as she stood waiting in the Salon for her next instructions. She was secretly pleased that she had known this information a week before the Duchess. Old Agatha was amazing. Verity decided to visit the Scullery every day to see what more information the old woman might have.

The Duke mumbled moodily, "I'll send Darcus with the invitation."

"No!" countered his wife. "Send that new young knight. His youthful enthusiasm will give a positive impression. Have him ask for a return reply." She paused. "Verity, darling!" she announced as if she hadn't known that Verity had been standing waiting for the last half hour.

Verity stepped out of the shadow, where she habitually stood when in the presence of the Duchess. She had developed a habit of this, for in her dark clothing she was virtually invisible to the Duchess and could pick up more information. Sometimes, the Duchess revealed intentions that were quite helpful to Verity's own plans. Verity realized she was really spying on the woman. Luckily, Euphoria was too self-assured to credit Verity with such cunning.

The Duchess smiled in contempt at Verity, who stood momentarily in the sun's beam. Verity shifted so that the sun wouldn't shine in her eyes. She glanced at a sudden movement from the Duke. He stared at her with an expression of mixed surprise and puzzlement. A glance from the Duchess, and he returned to his books. The Duchess frowned as if his puzzlement had transferred itself to her.

At least what ever thoughts she's thinking have wiped that look of contempt from her face, thought Verity.

The Duchess resumed her train of thought. "Verity you are proving to be of great assistance since we returned. It is just as well that you survived the river. Here is what I want you to do. Prepare the rear chamber for guests. We have added to our guest list."

"Yes, Milady," curtsied Verity, and left feeling a little contempt for herself. She was treated like a servant, but then her mother had done these assignments to manage the castle. "Perhaps that is the fate the Duchess has worked out for me. If so, it's not so bad. Better than being treated like a toad."

The reply to the Duchess's invitation came back promptly. At the Duchess's own request, the reply was read aloud by the messenger. She prepared to smile, but then...

We regret that we are unable to accept your generous invitation. We are entertaining close friends of His Majesty. Thank you kindly for the invitation.

Yours in God's trust,

Baron and Baroness von Balford.

The messenger left and the Duchess paced for an hour, venting her fury at having her invitation refused.

"How dare they?" she scoffed. "I will ruin them. I will see to it that his Majesty never speaks to them again."

On yet another occasion, thanks to Agatha's advanced information, Verity was in the Salon on some pretext at the critical moment when the Duchess demanded, "Husband! Do not just sit there like a stump. This is your humiliation too! A mere Baron is snubbing us—not for the King, but merely for friends of the royal family. Think of something!"

The Duke shrank further into his books.

"Milady!" said Verity.

"What is it, Toadie?" snapped the Duchess.

"I think I might suggest a solution to your vexing problem."

"And what might that be?" asked the Duchess, narrowing her eyes.

"Respond to the Baron with generosity. Re-invite them and include the King's favoured friends. That can only put you in favour with the royal family."

"Yessssss!" murmured the Duchess thoughtfully, looking at her husband. "It's a pity I have to work out such strategies without your assistance, dear Husband. Darcus?"

Verity shrank back into the dim corner before Darcus entered.

The Duchess smiled at Darcus. "My husband wishes to invite the Baron and his guests. Bring our young knight back, supply him with a fresh horse, and see him on his way with my husband's invitation." Darcus nodded and left.

Verity stepped forward as soon as he'd passed through the door.

"Verity, we'll put others in those back rooms. Prepare your parents' old chambers—the ones that face those boring fields to the south. They are the best we have next to our guest chambers where the Prince will be staying. Make certain there are good linens and fresh floors."

Verity nodded, curtsied, and departed.

Within a week, the Prince's arrival date was proclaimed and the Baron's acceptance was received. The fates were in motion and Verity had yet to see the Wizard.

𝔊hapter 30

HELP

The knock of hammers mingled with grunts and cheers as the workers raised the jousting tournament tents. Excitement grew as the fair grounds began to take shape, for it had been a long time since a tournament and fair had been held in Grenwoodle. Even the Duke was too occupied to dwell in gloom. At every opportunity, Violet and Verity watched the progress. This day, the girls had cleverly evaded the Duchess and her imposed tasks. The warm sun and smell of the meadow provided a relief from the tirades of Euphoria.

"The yellow gown looks very nice on you, Verity. Isn't it a relief to be almost done with our fittings?"

Verity laughed. "I was sure the seamstress thought I was a pin cushion." She changed her voice to one with a nasal tone. "Turn, Milady!" *Prick!* "Turn, Milady!" *Prick!* Verity turned and jumped with the words.

Violet laughed and clapped her hands together. "Oh, Verity, you are so funny! I wish… I wish…"

Verity stopped clowning and gently asked, "What do you wish?"

"I wish my life weren't such a mess."

The sound of galloping hooves came from the west road. Verity and Violet walked to the edge of the field to see who approached. It was a lone knight dressed entirely in black. He did not wear his helmet, but from where they stood, his features were indistinguishable. He appeared to be an enormous man astride a glorious steed. They watched as the Duke and several knights walked over to greet the newcomer. When the knight dismounted and faced the Duke, he towered over him.

From her childhood, Verity remembered a giant of a man who

had hung around Kailan. She also remembered gossip linking his name to her mother's. She started running toward him. Slightly perplexed, Violet followed. The men turned as Violet and Verity arrived and the Duke presented the girls who curtsied. The giant knight bowed to the two young ladies.

"Sir Bennefield," repeated Verity, astounded. She did remember him.

"Verity?" asked Bennefield, amazed. "The last time I saw you, I gave you a ride on my shoulders. Now look at you—all grown up!"

Simultaneously, they asked, "Where's Mother?" and "Where's Kailan?"

They paused to grin at each other.

"Where is my mother?" repeated Verity.

"She will see you soon. Have patience little one. What about Kailan? Is she in the castle?"

Verity and Violet exchanged a soulful look and stared at the ground.

Finally, Violet said, "She's gone..."

Bennefield gasped and whispered, "She's dead?"

"No, no! Not that!" Verity broke in, "She has gone to the nunnery."

"The—! I will return!" Bennefield mounted his destrier and galloped down the road without another word.

"That is a wonderful steed!" breathed one of the knights.

"And a fine knight!" stated the Duke, who turned and walked back to the jousting field.

As the girls walked back to the castle, Violet asked, "Do you think it's possible Kailan might return?"

"Unless she has taken her vows," worried Verity. "But wouldn't it be wonderful to see her again?"

From her window the next morning, Verity saw the raven. Rothko flew in circles over the garden in the early morning sunshine. She raced through the corridors to the back garden to give him a message for the Wizard, but he had already gone. Old

Agatha emerged from the Scullery with a basket. She walked over to the herb garden and bent to pick some chives. Verity strolled casually over to watch what she was doing.

"You saw the black spook?" cackled old Agatha, as she squatted in the garden.

"I did," replied Verity.

"Stroll around the jousting grounds this afternoon and you won't be sorry," grinned the old woman.

"It is a pleasant stroll. I shall do that," verified the girl, and she left the garden filled with anticipation. It was time to consult the Wizard and lay plans to thwart the Duchess so that Violet could have a chance for a happy life.

That afternoon, Verity found it difficult to get away from Violet, who wanted to talk about Lucien, Kailan, and Bennefield. Violet's moods swung rapidly between hope and despair; her mind was so agitated. Verity was beginning to think she would never get away when the Duchess entered Violet's chamber where the girls had just had the final fitting of their gowns. Euphoria carried a magnificent jewellery box. Verity rose from her chair and the Duchess swept over and sat upon it.

The Duchess spied Violet's gown still lying on the bed, and said, "There it is! Now we shall see what will enhance it. Jewels are essential, dear Violet."

Verity stepped to the other side of the bed. The Duchess looked at her disdainfully and pointedly said, "You won't be needing any jewels, of course. Don't you have something important that needs your attention, dear Verity?"

Verity curtsied. "If you'll pardon me, Milady, I have something important that needs my attention." And she withdrew, laughing to herself at how the Duchess's words were so true.

The jousting wall was still under construction as she strolled past that part of the tournament grounds. At least, she tried to stroll. She was walking as quickly as she dared without drawing attention to herself. She could see a figure under one of the large oak trees on the other side of the field where the woods began.

She was passing behind the armoury tents where the knights would don their armour for jousting, when Darcus stepped into her path. She stopped abruptly.

He smiled slyly, "Well, Milady Toadie! On the stroll?"

Verity gave a quick shake of her head and watched the man intently.

"Around this area," Darcus nodded his head toward the armoury tents, "a strollin' lady is fair game. It is assumed the lady is looking for something. So Darcus, being the gentleman he is, will be most happy to oblige Milady's desires."

Darcus stepped forward and seized the wrist of the hand Verity raised to protect her throat. He spun her around, put his arm around her waist, and drew her to him. Verity twisted her head away, screamed, and stamped as hard as she could on his instep. He laughed and kissed her neck. His grip strengthened and he pulled her head around by taking a fistful of hair and yanking on it until they were face to face. His breath was revolting. She closed her mouth, clenched her teeth, and squirmed to get away. He laughed scornfully.

"That feels good, Toadie. I like that. Keep it up!" and his laugh grew louder still. He stopped laughing to kiss her. His slimey livery lips had just touched hers when...

"That's enough, Darcus! Let her go! Now!" Darcus released her so suddenly that Verity sat down hard on a thistle.

Darcus bowed to the voice of authority and converted to the cowardly side of his character.

"She asked for it, coming down to the armoury tents like that," he whined defensively.

"This path travels past the armoury—not to it," said the Duke precisely, brandishing his sword, "and you, you scumbag, ambushed the child. Now be off with you, or I will be off with a part of you."

Darcus was gone as suddenly as he'd arrived.

Verity sat where she'd fallen and stared in bewilderment at the Duke. He looked more forceful than he ever had before now and the aura of command that he possessed was not merely from the new grey hair at his temples. However surprised, she still could not credit that it was he who had rescued her. The Duke put out a hand to assist her and she stood up.

"He has forced attentions on you before, has he child?"

"Yes, Milord, he has tried."

"I shall speak to the Duchess. He works for her. Pressure can be applied, but if you have any further problem, come to me. Is that clear?"

"Yes, Milord."

The Duke turned away, muttering to himself, "...blue, so intensely blue. She reminds me of my mother. The only person I've ever known with eyes so blue was my mother."

Verity paused to pick the thistle bits out of the back of her skirt before she hurried onward to the oak tree. The Wizard was sitting propped up against its trunk, snoring through his beard. Verity sat on the ground before him and looked up into the tree. There, Rothko the raven was snoring too. The bird stopped in mid-snore and opened one eye. He cocked his head for a good look at her. Verity gave a little giggle, looked back at the tournament grounds to be sure Darcus wasn't lurking, and resumed her position before the Wizard. He was looking at her—eyes wide open—as though he'd never been asleep.

"Hello," she greeted him, "I thought you were sleeping."

"I never sleep."

"You were snoring."

"I never snore—I only doze. Rothko must have been doing the snoring."

"Very well. We'll blame the poor bird," said Verity solemnly, but her eyes twinkled, and she winked at Rothko. Rothko accepted the wink as an invitation and dropped down on the ground next to her. He folded his wings neatly, sidled over to her, and leaned against her knees. Cocking his head, he said to the Wizard in a rough voice, "Pretty bird, pretty bird."

"You've made your point, you black rogue. I can see the two of you are friends. Now let's see what the pretty bird wants."

Verity talked as rapidly as she could. She had had time to prepare for this, and was as concise as possible, but she spared no details because she wanted the Wizard to help Violet.

She began, "It's about the Duchess…" Verity continued for a few minutes, "…and I conclude that the problem lies with those dreadful flowers.

"If the flowers' spell only made the Duchess feel good and confident, it could be used in Violet's favour, but her well-being is exaggerated. Her optimism is extreme and unrealistic. Her purpose is also unrealistic, but none can say 'nay' to her. If she is thwarted, she takes malicious glee in punishing the culprit who dares to disagree with her. Her mood swings are extreme. When the effect wears off, she becomes so irritable that none can say or do the right thing. And the punishments she puts out are cruel—far beyond possible consequences of the so-called crime.

"My plan is to destroy the flowers during the tournament. Then she will have only enough to see her through the Prince's visit, and afterwards, in time, she will become normal. What do you think? Could you tell me how to destroy the plants? I'm prepared to rip them up by the roots and burn them!"

The Wizard tugged at his beard as he thought. "When did she harvest her last supply?"

"Two days ago."

"How long will it last?"

"Until the conclusion of the Prince's visit, unless…"

The Wizard contemplated the ground as Verity chewed on a stem of grass. "Yes, unless the visit drags on, or she uses it too generously. Does Gregori use it too?"

Verity was startled to hear anyone refer to the Duke by his given name. She took a moment to reply, and the Wizard looked up.

"What is it?" he asked.

Verity did not answer his sensitive acknowledgment of her disquiet. She said, "Lord Grenwoodle may have tried it at some time—perhaps years ago—but I am fairly certain that he does not use it now. He seems to be consistently sad. His mood does not follow a pendulum. He rescued me today from Darcus's evil intentions. It would appear that he has some good qualities."

"Hmmmmm... interesting," replied the Wizard. His blue eyes were faded, but the expression in them was quite intense as he thought carefully.

"I will begin the destruction of the flowers. If I need help, I will send Rothko. You keep in touch with old Aggie and try to discover where the Duchess keeps her supply. It will probably be a white powder, and it wouldn't take much space. We may have to destroy it to weaken her. But if you locate it, don't touch it. If you were caught, she could seriously harm you. There's no guarantee that this will help Violet. You do understand, little one?"

She nodded. "There's another question I must ask you," said Verity with her eyes steadily on his face.

"Ask away," he replied.

"Who am I?"

There was a short pause before he replied, "You're Verity."

"Who are my parents?"

The Wizard looked a little surprised. "Your parents are Sir Frederick and Lady Prudence."

Verity noted that the Wizard did not use the past tense. He, for one, was sure they were alive.

"Then why am I disguised with soap that darkens my fair hair? And why am I presented as younger than Violet when I really think I may be older?"

"Let me answer your questions this way for now. Decisions were made for your protection. You are of good family and you are not being punished. All will be revealed, and, best of all, I can promise you that Lady Prudence and Sir Frederick will see you soon."

He held up a hand to stop her excited questions. "Ah, just be patient for a few more days," he paused. "Now tell me about that young man who almost shot your horse."

"How did you—?" Verity gasped.

Then she watched as Rothko flew up into the tree and ruffled his feathers. She nodded at the black messenger as he settled onto his perch.

She continued, "I don't know who he is, but it doesn't matter. I am certain I shall never see him again."

She turned away and walked back to the castle.

"Rumour has it..." murmured the Wizard to himself. "Come Rothko, let's see what we can do to make everyone's dreams come true."

Flap, flap, cracked the bird's wings through the deep shadows of the forest as he flew ahead of the Wizard's steady pace down the path toward the swamp.

Chapter 31

THE FIRST GUESTS ARRIVE

Verity's steps echoed down the long corridor. It was so quiet in the castle that for a moment she felt as if she were the only person alive within it. She stopped and listened. After a moment, she heard the Duchess bawling out some poor soul who had probably dropped a candle. She sounded very angry and loud, but distance muffled her words. She was in the irritable and harsh stage of her mood swings.

That's why it's so quiet in here. Everyone is lying low, Verity thought. *Well, I certainly don't want to meet up with her, but I must find her flower powder.*

She walked on. Where would the Duchess hide it? The Salon where they conducted estate business would not do. Too many people walk through there. She had been told to wait in there, unattended, many times.

The Tower! Perhaps it is unsealed now for Milady's own use. Verity approached the Tower corridor but the door was sealed and presumably locked. Discouraged, Verity walked away. Logically, the flower drug had to be kept in the Duchess's private chambers. Verity realized that made the most sense, but that also made her task much more challenging. How would she be able to enter the private quarters of the Duchess without raising suspicion?

The linens! She was being asked to supply and change linens in all the guest rooms. Would it be too much of a stretch to enter the Duchess's chambers on the pretext of changing her linens before the Prince's visit? The first thing to do was to ask Agatha when the last change was and when to expect the next change of linens. As Verity hurried to the Scullery, she crossed her fingers and hoped old Agatha could help, for time was running out. As she hurried, Verity wondered what was disturbing the Duchess this afternoon that had her in such a bad mood. Before Verity could reach the Scullery, she found the Duchess, or rather, the Duchess found her.

"Verity, there you are! Darcus told me you walked down to the armoury tents. You should know better than to visit the knights there. They might misunderstand your intentions."

"I did not go to the armoury tents. I was walking around the tournament grounds for a breath of fresh air!"

Verity knew better than to defend herself against a woman who considered herself always right, but it prickled that Darcus would bother to get her into trouble.

"Your excuses are not acceptable, Toadie. From now on, you confine yourself to the garden unless accompanied by proper escort."

"Yes, Milady."

Verity's heart grew heavy and discouraged. How could she carry out her plan now?

Trumpets sounded, announcing arrivals to the castle. Astonishment creased the Duchess's face. "He is not to arrive until the day after tomorrow. Come with me, Verity, so you may assist. Are the rooms ready for all our guests?"

"Yes, Milady. All is ready."

"Then let us greet our guest of honour. Stay behind me."

As they walked to the main steps, the squeak of the portcullis assured them that guests had arrived. The Duchess had the first glimpse of the incoming entourage. A note of relief coloured her voice. "Not His Royal Highness. It must be a neighbouring nobleman. Perhaps the Baron and Baroness. They wear the Italian red cloaks... No! It cannot be!"

Verity endeavoured to see beyond the Duchess. "What? Who?" She wiggled between the Duchess's clothing and the doorframe, and gasped, "Ohhhh!" She ran down the steps to the beautiful woman on a charming chestnut palfrey. The woman dismounted and held out her arms.

"Mother!"

"Verity! At last!"

Prudence and her daughter embraced tightly while tears trailed down their happy faces. Frederick handed their horses over to Garrod and drew his wife and daughter up the steps and away from the rest of their entourage. Then he, too, embraced his daughter. Verity thought her heart would explode with happiness, but then her happiness dissolved into fear as the cold voice of the Duchess intruded.

"So, you managed to return, Lady Prudence. Did you fulfill your mission? Where is the Florensi lace? Did you purchase the China silks? Was there any money left over from the purchases?" She sneered.

Verity let out a small sob of distress at the manner the Duchess showed to her mother, but Prudence smiled with satisfaction and climbed the stairs to meet the Duchess face to face. Frederick clasped Verity's arm to restrain her from following her mother. Verity's heart pounded.

Prudence reached the top of the steps and allowed her skirts to settle. She pushed back her hood and rearranged a stray lock of hair. Then she smiled broadly and in a clear, confident voice she said, "You may address me as Baroness von Balford. My husband Frederick is the son of the late Baron von Balford, who died extinguishing a mysterious blaze that began shortly after he entertained visitors. Witnesses suggest the fire was set deliberately."

The Duchess looked ill at ease and she would not look straight at Prudence, who continued, "The answer to your question is, 'yes.' Your lace, China silks, other fabrics, Venetian glass, and the rest of the list were purchased and are packed in the carts that are now passing under the portcullis. And here," she put out her hand, grasped the wrist of the Duchess, and placed three silver coins in her hand, "is the remainder of your money. If you desire more goods, you may order them through me. I can read and write French, Italian, and English, and I am now a dealer with accounts in several cities. Also," she paused on the word, "I brought you a painting from Rome—my gift."

Calmly, Prudence took a breath, watching the Duchess's face only, as the horses and carts continued to arrive. The Duchess looked grey. Verity was enjoying herself immensely.

Prudence continued, "Consider this remarkable and valuable painting an expression of gratitude for looking after my daughter." Turning toward Verity, she continued, "Verity looks very healthy, but that is a dull gown. Tch! Tch! We will have to dress you better than that my dear. But, to continue, dear Euphoria... "

Verity gasped at the familiarity her mother showed. No one ever addressed the Duchess by her given name. A lock of hair fell across the Duchess's face. She looked agitated. Beyond her, Violet had arrived, and, wide-eyed, was observing Prudence.

" ...our guests have now arrived. I shall introduce you."

A helmeted knight dismounted and assisted a man down from an enclosed, quite comfortable-looking cart. A flash of bright coral skirt gleamed as the man and the knight half-lifted a stout woman to the ground. They were heavily veiled from the dust of the road, and proceeded to bare their heads. The knight reached for his helmet. At that very moment, the Duke arrived from the Salon. After viewing the scene, he glanced at his wife. A tic fluttered her eyelid and she stared more intently. The Duke took her arm.

Prudence smiled. "May I present les Marquis et Marquise de Cortelaide, and their son, Sir Lucien de Cortelaide."

Violet flew down the steps and into Lucien's arms. Verity glanced back at the Duchess, who raised her chin defiantly. Her crimson mouth trembled in her pale face.

The Duke's mouth twitched and settled into a grin. "Welcome to Grenwoodle Castle. What a pleasant surprise! Do come in! Darcus! See to refreshments for our guests and have their chests taken to their quarters."

Darcus glowered with resentment. He was unaccustomed to receiving orders from the Duke. He looked to the Duchess for support, but she was staring dully into space.

"Frederick! Prudence! How delightful to see you again. You will be in your former rooms."

The Duchess stood shaking with shock. The Duke pushed her gently around and drew her to the Great Hall while he continued conversing with Frederick, shook hands with the Marquis, and kissed the ladies' hands. Verity watched in astonishment. What had happened to change the Duke? A flutter of black drew her eye. Rothko landed on an iron sconce nearby. He drew in his feathers, cocked his head, and winked at Verity. She laughed aloud as Violet and Lucien surrounded her and, taking her arms one on each side, pulled her still laughing into the Great Hall.

Chapter 32

THE MISSING YEARS

Verity couldn't imagine falling asleep after such an exciting day, but she dutifully went through the motions and, at length, blew out her candle. Her mind buzzed with the exciting stories of her mother's adventures. Her chest felt full of pride at her mother's accomplishments. Pride mixed with amazement at the discovery that her father was the new Baron von Balford—the long-lost son of the wispy, cranky, and crafty old Baron who had wanted to marry Violet for her money. Now, here was her father with his own money in ample supply, and the title and land. He was also a close friend of the Marquis—Lucien's father. Her head whirled and then settled on the private conversation she had had with her parents. Her mother had spoken of her fears for Verity.

"I was terrified the day I left, but I was certain that if I returned it would be the worse for you. I felt so helpless. Then Sir Bennefield and Garrod found me. Rather than return and put you in danger... I stayed away. You must understand, Verity. I didn't know why I was sent away, but I must have been a danger to you. You seemed to be safe with Violet. I still don't know why Euphoria took such drastic measures."

"Could it—?" Verity began. "It must have been the flowers."

Prudence looked puzzled. "Flowers? What flowers?"

Verity patted her mother's hand. "It doesn't matter right now. Go on, tell me what happened next."

"Sir Bennefield and Garrod accompanied me to Avignon where I took refuge in a convent. There, I learned what was on the list and was advised that the list was impossible. The items would only be available from distant cities and the money inadequate.

It only allowed for the purchase of a few of the items. Sir Bennefield told me he had sent word to your father convalescing at the Wizard's cottage. He said the gatekeeper was friendly to the Wizard and would let him know immediately. So we waited in Avignon for Sir Frederick to arrive. Meanwhile, with the help of a scholarly nun, I began to learn how to read and write. Then the first messages began to arrive."

Verity frowned. "Messages?"

Prudence grinned. "I don't know how he does it, but perhaps he is a Wizard after all. He began to send messages to me about you and your father. It was reassuring to say the least. I applied myself more enthusiastically to language and began to investigate the whereabouts of the items on the list. Then, mysteriously, I was invited to visit noble families living in Avignon. It seemed there was a certain Marquis who was a close friend of the Wizard, and the Marquis had sent letters of introduction for me to meet the important people of Avignon.

"Soon there was help available, and I began to locate the luxurious items listed. It became apparent that it was impractical to import only one bolt of embroidered silk all the way from China. With the guidance of a silk merchant, I ordered hundreds of silks, kept what I needed, and sold the rest. I began to make money and it multiplied rapidly. Garrod was a tremendous help once I taught him to read and write and especially do the figures. I wanted Sir Bennefield to return to Grenwoodle, but he would not leave me alone in a strange city.

"Then your father arrived. That was a grand day. He wanted me to return, of course. He preferred living near his crusty old father to keep an eye on him, even though they didn't get along. But we decided we should return in strength and in control. There was always a suspicion on your father's part that he wasn't wounded by an adversarial knight in battle, but by Darcus. We both feared that the plot to get rid of us had succeeded and we wondered what the motive was. Meanwhile, by the information sent from the Wizard, it was clear that you were well, happy in Violet's company, and in no immediate danger. We decided we could accomplish our task and return before you could be betrothed by the Duchess... and here we are!"

Verity nodded and grinned. "But Mother, what of Bennefield? Why did he stay once father was there?"

"For a while, we all assumed Kailan was still with you. Sir Bennefield still believed it when he returned. But then we noticed how many times the tutoring monk was mentioned. Brother Fancy, I believe?"

"Yes," Verity confirmed.

"Then one day, I asked Sir Bennefield to pick up and escort a shipment of glass from Venice. While on this task, he joined an Italian Duke's army and made a great deal of money for himself. He decided to stay a little longer so that he could ask Kailan to marry him... and did he?"

Verity shook her head. "Violet and I have not seen Kailan since you left. She entered a nunnery. Bennefield has gone there. I have not seen him since."

"Has she married the church?"

"I do not know." Mother and daughter looked soberly at each other. Then Prudence asked, "What flowers did you speak of?"

"Mother, I assure you that you were not the culprit being punished by the Duchess. It was I."

"You? You were only a child!"

Without hesitation, Verity told her mother about discovering the flowers and that the Duchess had threatened her. She explained about the wicked use made of the flowers. She also told her mother about her plans to destroy the source of the Duchess's malevolence.

Prudence covered her mouth with her hand. "My dear child, that is a dangerous plan. Withdrawal from her source of power could make her dangerously inhuman."

"Or destroy her. Or return her to a normal human being," added Verity.

"Why are you doing it now when she has plans to entertain the Prince? This is a critical moment!"

"If I may interject," said Frederick, to his daughter and wife, "I shall destroy the flowers for you. I can see that Euphoria plans to cause trouble for Lucien and Violet."

"Exactly!" agreed Verity. "She is determined to wed Violet to Prince Nicholas and she is so evil, she is even capable of harming Lucien. But Father, you do not have to destroy the flowers. The Wizard said he would do so and would send Rothko if he needed help."

"Rothko?" asked Prudence.

"His raven," explained Verity.

"The situation looks treacherous. I shall go warn the Marquis and Lucien," said Sir Frederick, and he reached for his sword.

"It is late," warned his wife.

"Their chambers are adjacent to our own. They will be grateful for the warning. I will return shortly."

Prudence followed him with her eyes as he left the room, and then she looked at Verity with a frown. "Where has the resident priest been during all of this evil? Does he not see what the Duchess does and how she acts? Is he not suspicious?"

"What priest?" asked Verity.

Prudence bit her lip and clasped Verity's hand. In silence, they waited for Frederick to return. The candle burned low. At length, the door quietly opened and he entered the room.

He said grimly, "Darcus has already tried to harm Lucien."

Verity gasped, "No!"

"No, he did not succeed. It seems Violet had already warned Lucien and they were armed when they opened the door. They put the fear of God into the little rodent and sent him scurrying away like the disgusting mouse he is. Come, daughter, I shall see you to your room and assure myself that you are safely stowed. Prudence, take my dagger and stay alert. I won't be long."

Prudence hugged her daughter. "Sleep well, dear child. In the morning, I shall dress you properly and we shall take you home with us."

Verity pulled away. "Mother, I cannot! I must stay until Violet is safely married to Lucien. There is no one to look out for her and I have both of you." She kissed her mother goodnight and joined her father in the hall.

Once settled in bed, Verity tugged the blanket higher and smiled in the dark as she remembered her father's reaction to her Garret Chamber. It was cold and dark, and he was horrified that there was no bolt. He quickly devised a temporary one from her single chair and his own girdle and sword. He lashed together the wood and the sword to a thickness that served, and then placed it so that she could shove it into place when he left.

"But Father, what of your own safety? Darcus may still be lurking in the unlit halls and you gave Mother your dagger."

"Do not fret, Sunshine," he grinned, and reaching up his sleeve drew out his snee, a short knife. "I would not leave myself unarmed." He kissed her and slipped out the door.

Verity slid the clumsy bolt into place and made ready for bed in the cold room. As she nestled into her bedclothes she thought of her father. It was so comforting to have his protection. She could sleep safely tonight.

She sat up with a jolt. "Sunshine?" She remembered when she was little. Her mother and father had called her "Sunshine." It seemed suddenly to be a vital clue. She snuggled down again and sleep beckoned at last, with blue eyes, fair hair, and an enticing grin.

Chapter 33

INTRUDER

Verity dreamed.

She lay on the pad and waited for his kiss. Though there was light from the fire, she couldn't see him. A rumble of sound and she felt afraid, but couldn't move. Was it the storm returning? Would she be swept away again? Another rumble, almost like hoof beats, but there was no horse. Again the sound.

She woke suddenly with her heart pounding. Someone was trying to open her door!

The moonlight trailed across the floor and just barely illuminated the base of the door. It moved again. The bolt rumbled in its place. Verity watched and prayed. After endless moments had passed, she moved her head, realizing she had been motionless for a long time while she listened. The intruder had gone. She lay back and stared, eyes wide, at the moonlight.

Chapter 34

A DAUNTING TASK

Verity awoke to a gentle knock. Pulling a blanket around her, she went to the door.

"Who is there?"

"Your mother," came a firm, calm voice.

Verity opened the door to put her arms around her mother. Prudence held her tightly and then motioned behind. Old Agatha came in grinning. She carried a tray of sweet buns and watered wine. The three broke their fast together in the Garret. Agatha could hardly eat; she was so awed to be there by invitation.

Verity took a sip of wine. "Father called me 'Sunshine' last night. I was called that when I was really small, wasn't I?"

Prudence looked at Agatha, who looked down. "Verity, don't tell anyone that. It was a slip of the tongue. Actually, a surprising one. I didn't think he remembered."

Verity noticed that her mother didn't caution Agatha.

"Mother, is my name really Verity?"

"Yes, dear."

"If 'Sunshine' was just a pet name, why is it a secret?"

"Let's just get through the tournament and the ball, and we'll sort out the rest when things settle down. Now, wash up, Verity, and come down to our chambers. Your new clothes are there. Agatha will stay with you and bring you down. What is your favourite colour, dear?"

"Blue!" answered Verity promptly.

"Oh, I think I left the blue one at the Baron's estate. Well, we'll find something you like, and Agatha will take it in. See you in a while."

After Prudence had gone, Verity said, "I didn't know you could sew, Agatha."

Agatha drew herself up straight and answered slowly, "I was once Lady's Maid and Dressmaker to the Grand Duchess of this very castle. She sent me, like a fine lady, to Brussels to learn the art of lace making. When I returned," Agatha wiped her eye, "the Grand Lady Annalynn was dead, and her son and his wife too…" Agatha paused, brightened, and continued, "I taught Prudence. She makes beautiful lace."

"I didn't know that," murmured Verity.

Agatha smiled, rose, and took Verity's hand.

"Now come, dear girl, let's prepare you for the tournament and make you beautiful for the Ball."

When Verity walked into her parents' chamber, she gasped at the beauty that filled the room. It looked as though a rainbow from the lake had floated into the room for a visit. Prudence had laid out dresses and fabrics so that the entire room was covered. Verity had never seen some of the colours before. She took a step further into the room and stopped. Eyes wide, she looked from one entrancing hue to another, enjoying the sensual pleasure it brought her. At last she let out a long sigh. Tears trickled down her cheeks. Prudence stepped over to her daughter and put an arm around her protectively.

"I'm very sorry, Verity. I should have realized it could be overwhelming. I have been surrounded by such beauty for so long… I just wanted to surprise you and please you."

Verity trembled. She tried to speak, took in a breath, and then in a shaky whisper, she pointed and said, "I never saw a green so brilliant. It's like the spring sun shining through the first leaves."

"Do you like green?" asked Prudence. "I noticed you wore green yesterday, and today as well, though a different gown."

Verity laughed. She laughed until her shoulders shook. She laughed as tears spilled down her cheeks. She laughed for such a long time that Agatha rubbed her back and Prudence rubbed her hands.

At last, Prudence said, "Agatha, pour some wine—full strength, old dear."

Agatha did and they managed to get a few sips into Verity. At length and at last, Verity calmed down. She started to hiccup. Agatha put some honey into the wine and coaxed her to keep sipping. Then the words began to pour out of Verity.

"It was when I discovered the red flowers—when I saw the demon in the flower. I fell back into the quicksand. She came and stood over me and screamed at me. Her hair was wild and grey in parts. She was covered in sweat and it rolled down her face like black tears. She looked like she had two black eyes. Her mouth was a ragged smudge of red, and her hands were covered in blood. She wouldn't help me out of the muck until I promised not to tell about the red flowers. She said I'd never see you again if I did tell you, and if I let out one croak about the flowers she would turn me into a toad. My hair is brown, my eyes are large, and she would only dress me in brown. I hated it, but I didn't complain. One day, she decided that a blue cast-off dress of Violet's would be more serviceable for me if it were dyed a darker colour, but that 'green would be more appropriate for a toad.' Deliberately, I frowned and looked as unhappy as I could. That convinced her that I hated green, so I've worn green ever since. It's really much nicer to look like leaves than like dirt, but I've never let her know how I feel. She calls me 'Toad' and derides me as often as she can."

Prudence smouldered with rage. She took a deep breath and then gently asked, "How have you managed to resist her abuse, remain true to yourself, and be as cheerful as you seem to be?"

Verity looked at Agatha, and then back to her mother. "Agatha can tell you. The Duchess has always been cold and unloving to Violet, so I tried to make it up to Violet by being as loving a friend as I could. By concentrating on her, I've been able to tolerate the Duchess. But... there have been occasions when I believed she was right, and I thought I did look like a toad so much that I could hop and croak. But then..." Verity's mouth curved into a grin. "One day, someone called me a 'Fairy Princess.' I asked him, 'Do I not look like a toad?' and he—seriously—said, 'No, you do not look anything like a toad. You look like a Fairy Princess.' Soon after I looked into a pool of water and saw that my hair was as fair as the rising sun. The brown colour had washed out when I was carried away by floodwaters. Mother, why must I wash my hair with a soap that turns it brown? Why am I disguised like a toad?"

"Oh my dear, brown hair doesn't make 'a toad.' You are not a toad. Don't listen to that wicked woman. You are…"

Trumpets from the ramparts interrupted Prudence. Mother and daughter looked at each other, eyes wide. "The guards have sighted the Prince's party. Quickly, Verity, put on a gown. Agatha! Which one do you think would fit her? I didn't know her size."

"Either the green or that bright crimson."

"Enough of green for my daughter. Let's try the crimson."

In no time, Verity was dressed and ready to greet Prince Nicholas in the Bailey. She was urged to go ahead. Agatha and Prudence wished to pack up the gowns and materials.

"We'll be down before he arrives," urged Prudence, "you go ahead. Show Violet your new gown. Enjoy yourself, Verity. It's tournament day! Time to enjoy the festivities!"

Verity ran down the stairs. She was so happy, she felt so light, and her tiny feet hardly kissed the cold stone steps. But as she rounded the last curve to the main floor, Darcus blocked her way.

"Toadie! My, my! All dressed up! You look like a toad who has been out in the sun too long! Where do you think you're going?"

"Let me pass. I'm going to join the household and welcome Prince Nicholas."

Darcus stepped closer. Verity shivered. He traced her jaw line with his finger, and when she turned her face away from his hand in disgust, he let it drop to stroke the top of her breast. She hit his hand away and tried to pass him. He grabbed her arm and held her still. "Not so hasty, Toadie. Your presence is requested in the Salon."

"Who asks?" retorted Verity, defiantly.

"Lady Violet!" he replied with a grin, knowing she would respond to Violet instantly.

"Please! My arm!" ordered Verity.

Darcus let go and raised his open hands. "Far be it for me to hold you up, dear little Toad, in your little red dress. Hop along now."

His laugh echoed up and down the circular stairwell. Verity turned and fled to the Salon. Before she opened the heavy great door, Verity reasoned how unlikely it would be for Violet to send Darcus for her, so she was not surprised that Violet was not in the Salon. Only the Duchess sat there on her great chair. Her jewellery box sat on the table in front of her. Verity looked at the box and then at the key that hung on a heavy gold chain around the Duchess's neck. She suddenly felt with certainty that she could now tell the Wizard where the Duchess kept her drug.

"Well! Well! Well! Look at our little toad. All dressed up for the tournament, is she? Your mother has a good time playing the fashion game, but the game is over, my amphibious pet! I have a task for you that cannot wait. Your mother has not mentioned one word about the red flowers. After all that effort I went to, it seems you never told your mother. Well, for such trustworthiness, there must be a reward, dear Verity. You have clearly won my favour and the privilege of doing me a great service. As you have no doubt heard, Prince Nicholas is about to arrive. It will be a glorious moment introducing my dear Violet to him. However, the past few days have been very trying for my delicate condition, and I have relied heavily on support from my beautiful flowers. You must go to the swamp and gather a new supply for me. Here," she lifted a basket from the floor, "are my tools."

Verity stared in horror at the basket. She stammered, "The P-p-p-Prince!"

The Duchess laughed, "What would the Prince want with a toad? You are insignificant, Verity—just a slip of a girl, and insipid at that. Not even a bright dress can help you! The Prince will, of course, choose Violet as his bride. She is tall, beautiful, and regal... while you are nothing. Now make haste and do as I say... unless... perhaps you will need assistance? Shall I call

Darcus? I am sure he would be happy to escort you through the woods."

"No!" Verity cringed.

The Duchess smiled. "Well...?"

"I will do as you bid, Milady. I will gather the..." Verity faltered, "th-th-th-the flowers."

"And bring back the basket full—just the heads!" the Duchess cackled.

Verity nodded.

"I cannot hear you!" snapped the Duchess.

"I will fill the basket with the flower heads," repeated Verity, tight-lipped. Tears coursed down her cheeks as she submitted to the Duchess's demand.

The Duchess passed the basket to Verity. With a sickening heart, Verity saw that the basket was much deeper than she had realized. Clods of swamp muck clung to the bottom.

"I'll change my dress," she murmured, remembering the filth of the swamp.

"No need for that!" retorted the Duchess sharply. Then she continued slowly, insinuatingly. "The flowers will appreciate the colour of your dress. Perhaps they will come more willingly to one dressed in crimson like themselves. Just think, Verity dear, perhaps they won't scratch you—as much." The Duchess's mouth curled into a menacing smile.

Verity looked at her enemy with mounting horror at the task she had accepted. She turned away just as the door opened and the Duke entered. He stopped abruptly, and looked fixedly at the expression of horror and fear on Verity's face. It was only a moment, but a shock of recognition ran through his powerful frame and he stood motionless as Verity passed, exited, and closed the door behind her.

The smile on the Duchess's face faded as she recognized the importance of her husband's shock. Gently, she guided him to a chair, brought him a cup of wine, and placed it to his lips. He sipped obediently and shuddered.

Quietly, the Duchess asked, "Did the red dress remind you of something, dear?"

"The blood," answered the Duke, picturing the wound in his father's side and his own sword stained in crimson. At long last, guilt crept into his heart, and he started to cry.

"Anything else, dear heart?" murmured the Duchess, rubbing his neck soothingly.

The Duke's inner eye travelled from his dripping sword to his father, and then to his brother's face frozen in an expression of horror and fear as he looked at their wounded father. "My brother," he whispered in horror as he realized, at last, that Verity looked exactly like his brother Stephen.

The Duchess narrowed her eyes in growing suspicion. It was time to ascertain Verity's birth. She straightened her shoulders.

"Immediately after I marry Violet to Prince Nicholas," she vowed, "I shall find out who the little amphibian really is. I have already discovered that the toad darkens her hair."

Clouds from a distant storm blocked the sunlight trickling into the room from the one high window. The Duke sat silently weeping.

Meanwhile, in the dim forest light, Verity's flowing tears blurred the once-familiar path as she ran carelessly through the woods. Her nimble feet were no match for the roots. Usually, the roots formed steps down to the meadow, but now they rose up, determined to trip her. Blindly, she stumbled repeatedly but continued her reckless pace until, on a sharp turn, she tripped on a menacing root designed to catch the unaware, and she was flung headlong down the treacherous path. As her body traced a crimson arc against the evergreens, she flung out her arms in protection and lost her grip on the dreaded basket. Flung up, it rose, spinning violently, before crashing into a high branch and dropping back to earth.

Verity landed with a thump in the tall grass on the edge of the path. The basket, now empty, hit the ground ahead of her with a crack, but a more menacing thump hit the ground next to her face. She opened her eyes in terror to see the throbbing blade of the Duchess's knife inches away. She rolled away from it, imagining for a moment that the Duchess herself had thrown it. She looked around frantically. A black shape hovered in the air above her. She let out a scream, but it was useless in the empty forest. The black shape slowly descended to the dusty ground.

Gradually, reason returned, and the forest's hush quieted Verity's racing heart. Slowly, eyes alert, she sat up. A soft murmuring breeze stirred the branches of the trees before ruffling the black cloth from the basket where it lay crumpled on the ground. It twitched and flopped, turning over and touching her skirts. She pulled them up and shuddered. The knife suddenly fell over in a small poof of dust, making her jump. As it rocked in the breeze, the basket uttered derogatory little creaks.

Verity still felt attacked by demons. Wide-eyed, she looked around the forest checking every bush, every stump, and every rock for wild animals, or worse—for the menacing shape of Darcus. Her ears magnified the forest sounds and forced her to check out every rustle. Finally, she felt alone and yet, as reassuring as that was for the moment, she was reluctant to stand up. Slowly, she discovered bruises and scrapes, but for the most part she was whole. She stood. Her new dress was torn; she choked back a sob. Controlling herself took more effort, and then the sun pushed away the clouds and the forest was brighter and less forbidding. It was time to gear up courage.

"I can do this," she said sternly to herself. "I'll get the flowers for the Duchess—they're just plants after all—and I'll take them to her. They will improve her disposition and she'll stop picking on me because she'll be engrossed with Violet and the Prince." She squinted up at the sun. "It's not even midday. I can return in time for some of the tournament—perhaps buy a leftover meat pie at the fair, because I will have missed the midday feast."

Verity gathered the cloth, knife, and basket, and once more set off down the path. This time with clear eyes and a level head, she soon found herself crossing the meadow to the swamp. But her troubles were not over yet.

Squinting against the sunlight, she looked across to the swamp. It seemed to be covered in white fog. She hadn't anticipated harvesting those horrible flowers in fog. After a pause, she trudged on with determination. After all, it was reasonable that sudden sunlight after showery weather would produce fog above a swampy area, but the sun should soon burn it off.

Giving herself courage, she spoke aloud, "A bit of fog isn't going to hold me up. I'll cut off their heads and be quick about it so I can return as soon as possible."

She was into the fog sooner than she expected as if it had advanced to meet her. It smelled foul, and she stopped abruptly. The fog swirled around her, thick and white. She covered her nose. Remembering the treacherous quicksand, she carefully checked the muddy ground ahead before taking tentative steps. All was not quiet in the thickening atmosphere. The fog hissed as it swirled.

"Surely, the wind will blow it away," she consoled herself.

The muddy quicksand sucked and plopped. She pulled aside her skirt and took a few more careful steps. A snake slithered away to her left. She shuddered and covered her nose against the overpowering smell of rot and decay.

"How many flowers can I harvest in conditions like this?" she asked herself, and then she saw the stalks.

Clusters of dead stalks stood white amid the acrid green swamp grass. Bent and broken stems, withered leaves, and shrivelled white flower heads lay in disarray around the bottoms of the dead stalks. Verity spun to her right. More white debris appeared out of the fog, which began to thin. She gasped and choked on the smell of death. Once more, she stepped forward. More white death. The once-crimson flowers had been destroyed. She picked up a white blossom head. The petals disintegrated in her hand and the ugly face had left nothing but a grinning skull. As her hands shook in repulsion, the skull disintegrated and blew away into the fog.

Verity felt giddy. She focused on the fog and could see floating particles. She waved her hand through it and collected the white particles, spilling them again into the air. It wasn't fog, she realized, and laughed. It was dead particles of the dead flowers hovering in the air. She stepped on a dead flower head. Up into the air rose a cloud of white smoke. It hissed. Verity laughed again and danced on the white stalks with a vengeance. Wet ground spattered mud and a dense white cloud enveloped her. She inhaled some of it and choked.

Horrified at what the poisonous cloud might do to her, she ran heedlessly toward a yellow shimmering light into the golden meadow. She stopped to look back; the white fog of the swamp undulated in its dance of death. Verity sneezed. A cloud of white dust came from her throat and lungs. One sneeze begat another until her blue eyes streamed. When the sneezing abated, she sat in the grass and pulled up her underskirt to wipe her face. Her face, hair, and dress were covered with the white dust and black mud. After a time, she picked up the basket and made her way back to the forest.

A black shadow of dread grasped her heart as she walked. She confronted her new predicament. She could not bring back the promised flowers to the Duchess, and she must be the bearer of the bad news that the flowers were gone. Would the Duchess assume she had destroyed them and kill her? Once again, tears trickled down her cheeks and sprinkled the ground as, with her head bent, she climbed up the forest path to the pond. Another black shadow traced circles behind her as Rothko followed her up the steep meadow. When she entered the forest, he flew straight and true to report all that he had seen.

Chapter 35

THE TOURNAMENT BEGINS

The Duchess smiled in satisfaction as she assessed the day. It was all going according to plan. Even the weather had cleared, bringing welcomed warmth to the spectators in the stands. The Duke seemed wrapped in melancholy, but she could tolerate his lack of interference with her plans quite nicely. While he brooded, she would accomplish her goals. She watched Prudence and Frederick. Prudence was looking everywhere except at the lists. She was obviously searching for Verity in all the wrong places.

"Ha! Stupid woman, to think she could outwit me!" murmured the Duchess.

She turned to watch Violet and Prince Nicholas. They seemed to be getting along quite well. Violet was even smiling now and then. The Duchess chuckled when she caught sight of Lucien frowning as Violet smiled at the Prince, who was evidently confiding something to her. When Lucien's turn at the lists was called, he galloped so fast to his position that his horse skidded and reared, bringing a gasp from the crowd. But then, when he unseated his opponent, a great cheer arose. Violet was on her feet cheering, but that was fine because the Prince was cheering too. The Duchess smiled again. Yes, things were going very well.

She looked around just in time to see a heavily veiled lady taking her place in the front row of the stands. Curiously, the priest, who had not visited the castle for some time, accompanied her. The Duchess shrugged and observed that the next two knights were getting into position. By his size, one of them could only be Sir Bennefield.

She smiled, "Maybe with my luck today, the brute will fall and break his interfering neck."

Chapter 36

PEARLY TEARS

For a long time, Verity sat by the pond, considering her options. Now and again, she wiped angrily at the silent tears still streaming down her face, but most of the time, she frowned in deep thought and ignored them. The disregarded tears rolled over the rock and into the water. They beaded together in bright incandescent light and drifted out over the pond like a string of pearls.

Verity concentrated on viewing the problem at hand. How could she awaken the Duchess's vengeance with the news that her drug-producing flowers had been destroyed? As the messenger of such tidings, she would put herself further in jeopardy. Perhaps she should run away. But she couldn't leave Violet. Not now. On the other hand, perhaps the Duchess had another source for her drugs. Perhaps the roots would regenerate. Perhaps without her drug, her precious drug, the wretched Duchess would turn into a nice lady.

"No chance of that!" she grimly said aloud.

"No chance of what?" queried a familiar voice.

Verity looked up to meet the steady gaze of the Wizard's faded blue eyes. Rothko sat on his shoulder and eyed her thoughtfully. Verity brushed away her tears. Two of them fell into the water and joined onto the string of pearls.

"Oh, I didn't hear you approach!"

"Why are you crying, my dear? It's such a foolish waste of pearls of wisdom," said the Wizard.

"What? I don't understand," she said as two more tears rolled down her cheeks.

The Wizard sat down on the rock next to her and gently let

the tears flow onto his fingers. The tears glistened and glowed, then rolled off his fingers and into the water where they joined the others.

"You see, my dear, you can't think so well when you cry. Feeling sorry for yourself just gets in the way of sensible thought. Now, you're a smart girl and not inclined to feel sorry for yourself, so there must be a problem bigger than you can handle. Tell us all about it."

"Where shall I begin?" Verity muttered to herself as she dried her face on her crimson skirt. The Wizard was right. It felt better to stop crying.

"Why don't you start by telling us how you became so bruised and dirty?" suggested the Wizard.

Verity looked at her crimson dress covered with white dust.

"The flowers!"

"What about the flowers?"

"They're white."

"White?"

"They're gone!"

"Gone?"

"They're dead, and when you touch them, they turn into clouds of dust—white dust. It's all over my dress."

"And in your hair," added Rothko with a squawk.

Verity touched her hair and felt the dust. She bent forward and looked into the pond. Ghostlike, her face looked back.

"I am a mess, aren't I?" she said soberly.

"You certainly are," exclaimed the Wizard.

"Verity's a mess! Squawk!" added Rothko.

"Tell me, Verity," asked the Wizard seriously, "why did you go down to the swamp?"

"The Duchess ordered me to gather the red flower heads for her drug supply."

"But Verity, you wanted the flowers destroyed, and I promised you I would do it for you."

Verity hung her head. "I didn't realize you would be able to destroy them so quickly. I thought they would be there until the end of the tournament. It has just begun today."

"Yes, well, it seems I was too efficient."

"It's my fault," said Verity. "I should have realized I couldn't outwit the Duchess or defeat her evil plans. Now she will truly become a monster and her first victim will be me!" She looked up into the Wizard's steady blue eyes. "I deserve it. I was too sure of myself and I am just a skinny little toad." She looked down at the rock and murmured, "Poor Violet."

"Violet?" echoed the Wizard.

"Yes." Verity looked up as Rothko jumped down and settled next to her on the rock. She reached out and gently stroked his feathers. "As I told you, Violet loves Lucien and the Duchess is determined to marry her to Prince Nicholas—and I can't stop her."

"I see. So you have decided to stop trying?"

"Yes—err, no! I just feel so defeated and I don't know what to do."

"In the first place, you should have more faith in your friend. Violet won't marry Nicholas if she loves another..."

"But her mother?"

" ...and in the second place, her mother is selfish and nasty, but she's not all-powerful. Everyone has weaknesses..."

"But..."

" ...and in the third place, the King's son won't be inclined to marry someone whose heart belongs to another. He just needs to be told."

Verity's face lit up with hope. She stood up and brushed off her dress. "You're right. I'll go find him and tell him. Now."

The Wizard rose and put his hands on her shoulders. "Hold on now. Not so hasty."

"Leap before you fly!" squawked Rothko, who flew up to a nearby branch.

The Wizard's eyebrows rose as he looked at the raven. "You mean, 'think before you leap,' rogue!"

Verity smiled, "Even better if you 'look before you leap!'"

"Now, look at you! Covered in dead dust and muck. You'd make a fine impression on the Prince. You have a nice bath in the pond. Then go to my cottage and rest. There's a tasty stew in the pot. Help yourself. Meanwhile, I'll go to the castle and replenish the old hag's drug supply so she won't miss the flowers."

"You have some of the drug?" asked Verity, wide-eyed.

The Wizard was dismissive. "Something close enough in appearance—different effect. Verity, think! Did you ever find out where she keeps it?"

"Yes, I'm fairly sure, but... it's impossible to reach!"

"Verity, just tell me. We're not defeated yet!"

"I'm certain it must be in her jewellery box. She keeps that near her most of the time and one day I saw it open when she showed Violet her jewels. The interior looked too shallow for the size of the box."

"Well observed, child." The Wizard stroked his beard.

"But it's locked, and she carries the key around her neck."

"Hmm..." mumbled the Wizard. "Simple enough. I shall persuade her to open it. Now, child, do as I say. Stay at the cottage out of sight. I will fetch you another dress to wear, and tonight I shall personally escort you to the Ball. Together, we shall make dreams come true... for Violet and Prince Nicholas."

The Wizard removed his cape and, with great strides, disappeared up the path to the castle.

All was quiet in the forest. Even Rothko had followed his master. Verity took off her clothes carefully so the dust wouldn't make her sneeze, and laid them in a neat pile on the rock. The Wizard had left his cloak. She touched its soft folds. *How thoughtful of him,* she mused, and then she looked into the pond. Knowing what had occurred in its water years ago, she pictured Kailan's straightened toe. She was a little uneasy at the thought of magic, but then with a shrug, she straightened her shoulders and dived into its pearly surface.

Chapter 37

A CHALLENGE AT THE TOURNAMENT

Prudence searched the crowd from her seat in the grand-
stand. Surely Verity's new red dress would be easy to identify. Isabella gave her a sympathetic glance and then tried to look
for Verity, too.

Frederick patted his wife's hand and said, "I'll check the stalls.
Perhaps she's eating a meal there."

Arthur the Marquis added, "She's probably shopping for some
trinket at the fair. Females love to shop in the fair. Isabella can
spend hours visiting the stalls for useless falderol. Hmph! I'll help
you look, Frederick."

As Arthur rose and followed his friend, he glanced over at
Violet laughing with the Prince. His mouth tightened and his
eyes sought Isabella's, but she seemed... indifferent? Indifferent
to their son's loss? Never! Maybe unaware—not Isabella, absolutely not. Or unconcerned? Arthur stopped at the edge of the
stand and looked back at his wife. She was actually unconcerned
about Violet and the Prince. That told him two things. One: she
knew something he didn't know. Two: whatever it was, she wasn't
worried. He grinned.

*So I don't have to worry either. Now, I must help Frederick find Verity.
Such a delicate little waif—reminds me of someone,* he thought, and
hurried to follow his friend.

Prudence chewed her lip. Where could Verity be? The Duchess
looked so smug about her success with the Prince. Prudence
clenched her fists in frustration and began to scan the audience
again. A joust ended with a knight hitting the ground with a
sudden thump. People stood and cheered the winner, and then
gradually settled. One woman, heavily veiled, made her way

through to the front and sat down. A priest followed her. The priest looked familiar, but then he pulled his hood over his head, which cut off Prudence's view. She scanned the spectators again, hoping to spot the red dress.

The Marquise touched her arm. "There! Isn't that Sir Bennefield?" she asked.

Prudence looked out to the lists. No one could mistake that bulk. "Yes, it must be," she answered shortly.

The jousting continued. At last, Frederick and Arthur returned. From their sober looks, Prudence knew they had not found Verity.

Isabella pointed to the lists. "Watch Sir Bennefield. He is winning."

The rapid pounding of hooves grew louder and with a great crash and thump, an armoured knight was unseated and hit the ground. The big giant rode the length of the lists, turned around at the end, and rode jauntily over to the stands. He waved a scarf of favour and dismounted. The veiled lady next to the priest rose and doffed her veiling as Sir Bennefield approached.

Everyone watched as the two embraced. The lady bestowed a yellow rose on the gentle giant and he, in turn, kissed her hand.

"It's Kailan!" cried Prudence, with a swell of emotion.

Sir Bennefield lifted Kailan from the stands and placed her gently on the ground. The two of them strolled, accompanied by great cheers, to the royal dais in the centre of the stand where Prince Nicholas, Lady Violet, and the Duke and Duchess sat.

The crowd hushed as Sir Bennefield, received by the Duke, raised an arm and declared in his booming voice, "Your Highness, Milord, Milady—my wife, Kailan."

"At last!" cried Frederick, who knew the aching that his friend had endured while waiting to be reunited with his love.

The cheering of the crowd drowned out the replies of the Duke and Duchess.

Isabella touched her face in awe. "He certainly is a popular knight."

"Yes, he is that," replied Frederick, "and she is well remembered, too. Look, here comes the Wizard."

Clad in soft earth-coloured clothes, the Wizard walked forward. His wide silver belt sparkled in the afternoon sun. His hoary grey locks ruffled in the breeze as he stood at the edge of the stand and looked steadily in the direction of the Duchess. The Duke, his eye caught by the glint of the sun on the silver belt, looked at the old man and then at his wife. After several long seconds, as if drawn by the Wizard's stare, the Duchess slowly and deliberately turned and returned his gaze. More seconds dragged by slowly. Time seemed to take a rest as a hush fell over the crowd. The mounted knights in the lists stared at the Duke and Duchess, waiting for their signal to begin. They waited in vain, watching the Duke watch the Duchess watching the Wizard. The crowd's focus shifted from the lists to the Duchess. It seemed as though the Wizard's spell had immobilized her spirit. She sat motionless and unblinking.

At last, the Wizard broke his hold on her by grinning broadly. This seemed to infuriate her. Colour rose in her face and her fists clenched. She spoke to the Duke and gestured impatiently at the lists. The Duke gave the signal and the tournament continued. When the Duchess looked back toward the Wizard, he had disappeared. Gone was the Duchess's smug demeanour. Disquiet settled on her like a cloud. Prudence observed the entire interchange of wills and the deflation of the Duchess's confidence. She could not have explained why, but Prudence instantly felt relief. Irrationally, she was sure the Wizard's presence meant that Verity was safe.

Prudence leaned over to Isabella and asked, "Did you observe?"

"Yes, I saw," smiled the Marquise. "The Duchess doesn't have everything according to her wishes. And, the Wizard exudes more than his usual confidence. That was akin to a challenge and she did not take it well. I wouldn't worry about Verity, Prudence. I'm sure she's fine."

Prudence smiled at her friend. Frederick and Arthur, observing their exchange, were also relieved even though they couldn't say why. All four continued to look around the crowd for the red dress.

Chapter 38

THE HIDING PLACE

His legs were still strong for his years, and the old man rapidly made his way to the Castle Keep. He entered by the portcullis, greeting the vigilant gatekeeper, who never refused entry to the Wizard. The castle was next to empty. That made his search less complicated and much faster. First, he checked the Salon—the private room of the Duke and Duchess just off the Great Hall. Of course it was locked, but locked doors were never a problem for the Wizard, who had a magic key that would open any lock. It took mere minutes to ascertain that no cupboards or hidden chambers held the Duchess's jewellery chest. That left her private chamber. He mounted the stairs two at a time.

Even in daylight, the passageway was dimly lit, but the Wizard did not hesitate until he came to a corner. Straight ahead was the passage to the Tower. It was more than locked. Timbers were nailed across the door. The chest would not be there. He turned right and walked straight to the Duchess's Chamber door. His magic key whispered as it slid home, and in a moment he stood within, staring at the heavy opulence and feeling the room's sinister atmosphere. Faint whispers touched his ears. He strained to hear their source or meaning as they rose and fell, but he could not. He felt as if he was being observed and, looking around, he turned cautiously. Behind to his right, he was startled by a figure, but it was only his own reflection in an enormous and elaborately framed mirror, freestanding in the corner. Composing himself, he began to search the room methodically.

He began with the mirror. Supported by a heavy and unusually shaped base, the mirror rocked back and forth at the slightest touch. His fingers rapidly touched the base, looking for a lever or catch to open a secret compartment. The carved base was large enough to hold the jewellery chest that Verity had described, but he could find no means to open its thick sides.

He next tried the bed. It was high and had plenty of room below for storage. Such an obvious place should not be overlooked. He moved quickly and in a few minutes had completed that inventory. In the corner was an ebony wardrobe. He opened it to reveal the Duchess's extensive and elaborate collection of richly embroidered and beaded silk gowns. One gown of deep burgundy was heavy with sparkling brightness. He looked closer and saw diamonds on the neckline. He sighed and continued his search, trying not to think of the peasants who almost froze during the last winter. He already knew the Duchess cared little for the welfare of her dependents and overruled the Duke's decisions.

He tried the chests and chair. He looked behind the bed's drapery. He checked the walls for secret niches. He was closely inspecting the floor when he heard approaching sounds coming from the hall. He slipped behind the bed's drapery and pressed himself flat to the wall. He slowed his breathing and tried to shrink. A tiny hole in the drapery, thanks to the foresight of a beneficent moth, gave him an excellent view of most of the room.

The door opened. The Duchess swept in as the Duke held the door. No servant accompanied them, but the Duchess held the very target of his search—a carved chest. She spun around to continue an argument with the Duke.

"You have no idea of the danger that man represents. You're a poor excuse for nobility. You have no instincts, no skills of observation, and no deductive abilities. Everything depends on me!"

The Duke's face looked patiently strained. "The Wizard has lived here in the woods since I was a child. He has never defied our rule. He has never interfered. I'm sure he doesn't even care what we do. You are upset over nothing. It was a pleasant afternoon. He was enjoying himself. He merely laughed, my dear, he merely laughed."

Behind the drapery, the Wizard bit his lip.

"He laughed at me! Do not belittle what he meant. It was a challenge!"

"You see ferrets where there are merely rabbits. What are you going to do about it?"

The Duchess shoved the chest at her husband. "Put this away. I must prepare for the Ball. Where is Verity with my precious flowers? I have to prepare the powder."

"Verity is reliable. She'll be here."

The Duke carried the chest to the left—just out of sight. The Wizard chanced a slight move of his head to see between the drape and the wall. He could only see part of the stately mirror and part of the Duke's figure growing larger as he approached it. Suddenly he shrank, and the Wizard guessed the Duke had stooped or bent over. A grasping sound indicated a wood-on-wood movement. The Wizard leaned to the left to see better. The drapery rustled softly.

"What was that?" said the Duchess sharply.

"What was what?" asked the Duke with a touch of exasperation.

"That whisper."

The Wizard held his breath. One moment dragged on to two, and then three.

"My robe sleeve caught on the frame," the Duke said to appease her, as was his habit. He came back into the Wizard's view and put his hands on his wife's shoulders so suddenly that she flinched.

"You need something to settle you. Are you certain there is no powder left in your jewellery chest?"

"Not enough for the Ball. I must be at my best!"

The Duke pushed her back to the bed. "Rest now. I shall find Verity and make your powder. Try to calm yourself. I may have some of mine left. I'll look. I'll bring you some of it."

"Rest! Calm! You bore me, Gregori! I need excitement—not rest! Tonight's Ball is crucial to my plan. We shall be connected, indeed related, to royalty! Don't you see?"

"Yes, yes, yes, I see what you wish to do. But Euphoria, my

dear, you cannot force the Prince into a marriage and you must not force your own daughter. She is fond of Lucien. She may not agree to marry the Prince."

"Gregori! You are giving me a headache. Go! Get my powder and tell Verity she is forbidden to go to the Ball. As mousy as I've forced her to be, she is still attractive to men. Look at Darcus—he cannot leave her alone. It will be far easier if she were not there so that Violet can shine in her moment of glory!"

She raised her hands in a grand gesture, and then fell back on the pillow. The Duke patted her arm.

"I'll be back soon. Just rest." He hurried out.

The Wizard breathed very slowly and contracted his muscles one at a time so that he could stand very still.

The Duchess began to mumble. "Rest. Rest. Boring, boring, boring! I shall put an end to Verity before she ruins ev-er-y-thing."

She sat up abruptly. "Someone is in my chamber! Come out, you coward. I know who you are, Annalynn! Fair of face. Dainty yet your big eyes haunt my chamber again. You never let me rest. Leave my chamber. Be gone!" She fell back against the pillows, while a ragged sob escaped her mouth. "Gregori is mine," she whispered, "you merely gave him birth. You're dead now. Leave us in peace."

The Wizard sighed in pity, in spite of his iron control.

The Duchess sat up again, "Sigh and be gone, you persistent apparition. Haunt someone else. Leave me alone!"

The Wizard blinked. There! In the opposite wall a crack appeared, slightly opening as if it were a door. Luminosity passed into the room. Fair of face, its glowing hair floated in the air. Small hands pleaded and entreated, "What?"

Glowing eyes like blue flames of ice animated the sorrowful face. Closer it came, approaching the bed. The eyes grew larger still.

Euphoria raised her hands to protect herself from the sight and then suddenly, with a choking gasp of, "Don't touch me!" she fainted.

The apparition then looked straight at the Wizard. The sad

expression in her eyes brought tears to his eyes—tears that coursed down his grizzled face and blurred his sight. He blinked. The apparition was gone and the wall was closed as before. The Wizard moved quickly from behind the drapery and turned to the mirror. The heavy base was now solid in the centre. The jewellery chest fitted into the frame as part of the whole in plain sight.

"So, you revealed all—just as I thought you would," he whispered to the unconscious woman on the bed. He opened the chest with his key, found the lower compartment, and examined it closely. Dust clung to the edges. He dug into his robe, pulled forth a pouch, emptied it into the compartment, and closed the chest silently. Without a glance at the Duchess, he quietly left the chamber unseen.

Chapter 39

READY FOR THE BALL

Smoke curled crookedly upward as wispy breezes from the lake sifted through the woods and swirled it to and fro. Below the chimney, the stone cottage glowed through its windows in the early evening dusk. Inside, the broom moved to and fro as Verity, singing in her clear, sweet voice, cleaned the cottage. Once she had tidied, dusted, and scrubbed, she could see it was a comfortable home. She stored the broom in the chimney corner and sat in the chair to inspect the effect of her efforts.

Her fingers twisted a lock of her now fair hair. She looked at it with a touch of wonder, and memory surfaced once again: his fair hair brushing her cheek as he bent to see that she was breathing. She recalled his strong jawline faintly stubbled with fine hair. The dimple in his chin broadened slightly when he smiled. His blue eyes twinkled in delight that she was truly alive. Verity tried to hold the clear image of him as she had first seen him, but his image faded as if rippled by waves of thought—disturbing thought. The image of the Duchess took his place. Her hands stretched out with her palms up. Her eyes demanding as she glared at Verity. Verity covered her face with her hands and cried.

"Now, now, didn't we agree that feeling sorry for yourself is detrimental to thinking positively?"

Verity dropped her hands and rushed into the Wizard's arms. He hugged her until she stopped shaking, and then asked in an indignant tone, "What on earth happened to my cottage?"

Verity looked around as if things had changed since her waking nightmare. She grinned, "I straightened it up and gave it a good cleaning." Then she spotted a pile of shimmering blue material. It was the colour of the sky on a clear September day. "Ohhh, isn't that beautiful?"

"Not as beautiful as it will be once you put it on. Come now—do be quick. We must get ready for the Ball. I promised I would escort you. I will go to the pond to freshen up, and together we'll enter the Great Hall. The old Duchess will be so stunned she might even keep her mouth shut."

So saying, he lifted some clothing for himself from the wall hooks and left. Verity took off the shawl she wore over her chemise and slipped on the shimmering blue dress. It fit her perfectly. She looked down at the hem. The length was just right. Her mother had guessed the size correctly on this dress. Her hair fell forward and she brushed it aside as she looked. Then she noticed it was uncombed and tangled. Somehow she must dress her hair to be appropriate for her new gown. She looked around for a comb. She remembered that, as she had dusted, she had seen an odd-looking grooming chest next to the books. She stood on a stool and brought the chest down to the table. It was exquisite with inlaid parquet and carved sides. Inside were a bone brush and comb, smooth and pale. They were simply beautiful. Under a blue cloth, she found a matching hand mirror. She set to work at once and soon had her hair untangled, smooth, and glossy.

Behind her sounded a *flap, scratch,* and, "Awk! Pretty girl!" Rothko cocked a beady eye at her from the windowsill.

Verity laughed. "You're a flatterer, dear bird, and I love you for it. Isn't this dress beautiful?" She turned around in a pirouette.

"Awk! Pretty! Annalynn!" squawked Rothko.

Clap! Clap! Clap! Applause came from a dignified stranger at the front door. "You're right, you rogue, she's Annalynn!"

Verity's eyes widened in surprise. The Wizard in noble clothes—dark, rich blue, and edged in silver. He had tidily trimmed his beard.

After a moment, Verity regained her senses and said, "You look wonderful!"

"Thank you," he grinned.

"Do you have a name, Sir Wizard?" Verity asked solemnly.

"Yes, I do. But I buried it a long time ago. To be anonymous provides mystery. For tonight, I shall remain 'Sir Wizard,'" he grinned and added, "Just as you say."

She grinned back and quickly asked, "Who is Annalynn?"

"Someone I was very fond of…"

"Squawk!" Rothko interrupted and impatiently shifted from foot to foot on his perch. From his beak dangled a long blue ribbon.

"Thank you, Rothko," Verity caught the ribbon as her feathered friend dropped it and, twisting her thick long golden hair up above her head, tied it with the ribbon and pulled the waves around in a loose hairstyle. She looked into the small mirror. "Is that satisfactory?"

"Perfectly," answered the Wizard. "Where are your shoes? You cannot dance at the Ball barefoot. Someone might step on your toes!"

Verity picked up her shoes by the fire, where she had placed them to dry out. "They're still wet. I shall have to squish!"

The Wizard exchanged a look with Rothko. "I may just have something." He went to a chest in the corner and brought out a pair of silvery shoes.

"Oh!" gasped Verity, as she tried them on. "They fit me! They are exquisite! Where did you…?"

"You still need the finishing touch," said the Wizard, and from within his doublet, he brought out a string of pearls. "These will remind you that tears are a waste of time. Now you can smile when you dance with the Prince."

Verity smiled through tears of wonder glistening in her eyes.

As the Wizard fastened the pearls around her neck, she promised, "I shall take good care of them. Thank you for letting me borrow them. Did they belong to Annalynn?"

"Yes, and before—when time began—to her mother. Now, let us go to the Ball. Come, Rothko!"

Chapter 40

MOTHER KNOWS BEST

Inside, the castle preparations for the Ball continued as last-minute guests from neighbouring castles arrived at the gate. The Marquise Isabella was trying to dress, but she was frequently interrupted. In chemise and cotte, Isabella sat before her mirror, while Fiametta dressed her hair. Pagley interfered with unwanted instructions.

"Belle! Belle! I can't find my black hose." Arthur strode into the screened corner where the women had thought privacy was theirs.

Pagley deliberately shifted her weight to block him and, naturally, he did not see her, because she was short and he looked over her. The collision caused the Marquis considerable distress.

"Oh, Pagley, I am so terribly sorry! I did not notice you there. Did I hurt you?"

Pagley turned her head slightly so he could not see her grin of satisfaction, but Isabella caught it in the mirror.

Her mouth twitched in humour but her voice was steady and quite equable as she answered, "Did not Mortimer lay out everything in order for you, my pet?"

"Yes, yes, of course, but I wish to wear the black hose—not the blue."

Isabella's head bobbed back and forth as Fiametta vigorously brushed her hair. Fiametta's vigour increased as she fought the urge to laugh.

Isabella raised her hand and restrained Fiametta's arm. "My dearest Arthur, if you wish to mix colours, then that is of no concern to me. But I do think dark blue hose would set off the blue brocade you plan to wear, and that would indeed enhance your manly figure."

Arthur sucked in a short breath. "I see, I see. You're perfectly right, of course. I only want to look my best. I'm glad I asked." He bent and kissed his wife and left, most satisfied.

Fiametta continued brushing Isabella's honey-hued hair. Pagley prepared the hennin, a tall golden cone, for Isabella's crowning touch. She attached the veil carefully to it so that a brushing touch would not disengage it. She still had a small smile on her lips. Fiametta held her breath and swooped up the Marquise's heavy hair, fixing it carefully with combs and pins that she held in her teeth.

She sighed and, as the heavy hair settled into place, she nodded. "If you would like to assume your gown, Milady, your hair is in place."

"Good, Fiametta, I don't want to be late. I want to be close to Lady Prudence. She is anxious about Verity."

"What is the matter with Verity, Mother?" Lucien had come in, totally unannounced.

Isabella and her two maids turned in surprise.

"Nothing! I'm sure she's fine. Lucien! You're not ready yet!"

"I'm as ready as I want to be to sit and watch that fish dance with my flower!" So saying, Lucien sat in a huff on the floor and shut his eyes.

Isabella glanced at her two girls who disappeared as silently as candle smoke.

The Marquise regarded her son soberly. "Prince Nicholas is your best friend. Unnecessary jealousy is not a flattering cloak, Lucien."

Lucien opened one eye and squinted at his mother. "I'd like to see you tolerate Father dancing with the Duchess all night!"

"If it were necessary, I'm sure he'd smile and make the sacrifice," retorted the Marquise. "Pouting makes a poor liripipe."

Lucien continued to squint up at her. "If I could be sure that Violet's smile were equivalent to Father's theoretical smile, and that she continued to hold my face in her heart, I would not falter."

"Then go and dress, my son, because the only one in Violet's heart is you—no matter how she seems to attend to the Prince."

"How can you be sure?"

Isabella smiled gently at her son and ruffled his unruly hair. "Trust me! I'm a mother."

Lucien grinned.

"Belle, Belle! My hose has a hole." Half-dressed, Arthur padded in with one big toe exposed through dark blue wool.

Isabella called, "Pagley!" Pagley came as if from nowhere, armed with her sewing basket. Isabella strolled out of the corner on the arm of her son. The two looked back at the Marquis now sitting on the low stool Isabella had vacated. His foot extended forth to where Pagley knelt, intently sewing up the hole. The dubious look on the Marquis's face brought grins to mother and son.

"Will she stick him?" whispered Lucien.

"No doubt—just a little," whispered back his mother.

Lucien went out the door with a wave and a wink to her. She smiled and gratefully submitted to Fiametta, who helped her mistress dress in golden brocade.

Chapter 41

THE POTION

In the Grande Chamber of the Duchy, Euphoria woke from her faint, feeling groggy and disoriented. She looked out the window. Pale light still glimmered on the wall, but it must be late. She sat up. There, ahead, she could see traces of pale powder on the floor before her chest. Relief washed over her. The chest drawer was ajar. He must have replenished it without waking her. Gregori had been so sure she needed rest.

"Lovely powder—my magic friend—you are all I need."

Eagerly, she prepared her usual draught, pouring a colourless liquid from a covered beaker hidden in the mirror's base into her silver wine cup. White powder sizzled as it touched the liquid. Spiralling down, the powder dissolved, turning the liquid a pale red at first, before growing darker and darker. As bright as blood it swirled and the Duchess's eyes gleamed in anticipation. As she watched, the colour deepened. She raised one eyebrow in surprise.

"A powerful batch, my little beauties. It pays to let Verity harvest my precious flowers. Wouldn't it be a pity if the poor little toad was too scratched up to attend the Ball?" She chuckled to herself. "No matter! If she attends tonight to spoil Violet's triumph, I shall ensure hers is a brief appearance."

Vapour rose from the wine cup and settled as a red cloud above the rim. The Duchess sniffed appreciatively and smiled.

"Ahhh, my magic friend, you are the centre of my being!"

She began to chant:

Fountain of my youth and
Essence of my beauty,
Be my strength and give me life
As is your duty.
Origin of cunning,
Familiar Spirit, Hear!
Babble up to make me Sorceress,
Wicca without peer.
Source of my vitality,
Source that rules mortality,
Rise in all fertility,
Give me power over all!

The red cloud rose and spread. She closed her eyes and drank the potion down. She cradled the empty cup against her breast as the swelling cloud engulfed her figure. As if a thousand demons were released, it spun around her in a shrieking frenzy. Glowing in the red haze, her hair and gown twitched as if touched by unseen forces, but she remained sated and still in the eyes of the storm.

Gradually, the tempest spent itself and the room grew as quiet as a tomb. In her mind, Euphoria was a small child once more. Her mother had her by the hand and they were in her mother's tomb. She remembered being frightened of the place because it was dark, but her mother coaxed a candle into life and told her she could play there anytime. Her mother then pulled some flowers from her basket and showed her daughter how to produce their magic potion.

That was the first day Euphoria had tasted the power and the beginning of her devotion to its dual effects. No longer was she obliged to duty, especially duty to others. She was free of ethics and kindness, insensible in the portion of her mind that might consider other people's needs or feelings. As much as she forgot those considerations, the rest of her mind was stimulated and her ambitions grew. Desires became needs, and she pursued them relentlessly and ruthlessly. It became easier to achieve anything she desired, because she was unhindered by conscience. Her mother had smiled at her progress.

Euphoria smiled to herself now as she reflected on this memory and then she frowned as another picture emerged. She was introducing Violet to the magic potion. Violet had looked at her with frightened eyes, just as she had in her own childhood. At first, Violet tried a sip, but caution ruled her childish mind, and she refused to finish the draught. Euphoria had kept her patience and gave her more another day.

"I don't like it, Mother. It tastes bad, and when I drink it, Verity doesn't like me."

"Verity doesn't matter. This is good for you. Drink it."

As tears rolled down her cheeks, Violet took a sip. She made a face and slapped away the cup, "No more!"

That was the day Violet had deliberately spilled gruel on Verity's new dress when Verity received undue attention. Prudence had tried so hard to remove the stain and Euphoria remembered how triumphant she felt. That was the day Euphoria had planned that Verity would always wear peasants' colours while Violet would wear royal colours. But Violet never again drank the potion.

Euphoria opened her eyes and shrugged. "Never mind," she assured herself. "When she marries the Prince, she will see how ruthless one has to be in the political court. She will change her attitude. I'll see to that!"

A soft knock at the door roused the Duchess from her thoughts. It had grown dim in the room.

"Come in!" she called, and her servants entered with towels, basins, and lit candles. She would have to hurry before her guests arrived. She began to issue orders.

Chapter 42

PREMONITION

Agatha plaited Prudence's heavy chestnut hair as she watched her mistress twisting her rings in agitation. Gone was the confident woman who had returned from Italy. Prudence could hardly sit still for the necessary time it would take to produce the ornate braiding so stylish in the southern climes.

Agatha's own grey hair had been braided and re-braided as a result of her hours of practice to achieve the style that Prudence desired. Unlike Prudence's hair, Agatha's had grown quite thin, so she had brushed it back, braided the ends into an elaborate bun shape, and covered it with a wimple to avoid ridicule from the other servants. Agatha began to talk in a low, soothing voice to calm Prudence.

"The crimson looked so pretty on Verity. She's having a lovely time, I'm sure, and I will help her dress for tonight when she returns. She's probably with Violet right now. Those two are like sisters, they are. Everything will work out, ye'll see."

As Agatha continued, Prudence relaxed a little. After a while, Prudence interrupted.

"Agatha, dear friend, thank you for the reassurances about Verity. I knew this day at the tournament when the Wizard laughed that the Duchess did not have Verity, and I'm sure she's safe at the moment. I am also confident that she will attend the Ball tonight. But, Isabella is certain that Violet will not accept the Prince's proposal, because of her love for Lucien. You know the Duchess. You can guess what could happen when Violet refuses the Prince. I have a strong premonition that some horrible disaster will occur tonight. That is why I am agitated. That woman is capable of anything. Revenge in her hands would be of the cruellest kind. This premonition of mine is telling me that Verity may become involved and she is so young and vulnerable."

"But ye will be at the Ball, Milady. If a disaster occurs, remove yer child from the scene. You have confronted the Duchess and won before. Your shining goodness can surely prevail again!" Agatha's breath grew short and her cheeks grew pink as she staunchly supported her friend.

Prudence smiled and patted Agatha's arm. "Never fear, dear Agatha. I will do anything for Verity."

Agatha took a deep breath and let it out in a burst of indignation, "And besides, if the worst happens, ye have Sir Frederick by ye, straight and tall. I'm sure the two of ye can keep Sunshine safe from the Duchess."

There was an awkward pause. Prudence held her breath in shock. Agatha bent and concentrated on the last critical placement of the braids that now formed circular patterns in the air over and behind Prudence's head.

Then Agatha put her hands firmly on Prudence's shoulders and bent to whisper in her ear. "I mean 'Verity,' of course."

They looked at each other in the mirror, in silent understanding.

Then Agatha straightened and declared, "Ye look beautiful. It is time to dress. I am pleased ye chose the green silk. It shows off yer warm skin."

Just as Prudence was completely dressed, as if on cue, Sir Frederick entered the chamber. The setting sun streamed in the window and caught Prudence fully, just as she turned for Agatha's critical appraisal.

Frederick gasped, "There can be no one in the kingdom more lovely than you, my dear!"

Agatha glided past Prudence like a swan, muttering so that only Prudence heard, "Straight and tall beside ye all the way. Never fear the Duchess's tricks. The pair of ye can handle that old harridan."

Prudence smiled, "And you, dear husband, straight and tall and handsome in your finery."

They embraced. Frederick gently kissed her neck and then her ear. He moved back a bit, looking at her shining braids in their intricate pattern.

"The Duchess will be as green as your dress when she sees you tonight. I anticipate sparks with glee."

Prudence smiled at his mischief. Then she said soberly, "Stay close to me, dear Frederick. Help me guard our sweet daughter. For tonight, I have a feeling that havoc is on the program and the Duchess will be at her worst."

"Never fear, dear one. We are ready."

"We?" Prudence questioned with a sharp look.

"Yes, my green-clad lady, we are not alone anymore," and he extended his arm to her with a smile.

"Then let us be off, dear Frederick, and face the Dragon Lady in her lair."

They left the room.

Chapter 43

THE CHARADE

The gloomy expression on Prince Nicholas's chiselled face did not suit him. His face was meant to smile. His lean, muscled body slumped against the window shutters with his head drooping. His eyes stared at the scene below, unseeing. A short, sturdy figure in black bustled into the chamber carrying silver footwear for his master. He paused and contemplated the young man's obvious melancholy.

"Your Highness!"

Nicholas turned, acknowledging his servant in a flat, disinterested, but civil tone. "Yes, Walther."

"Your dancing shoes are repaired." He held them up for inspection.

"Fine," was the abrupt answer. Nicholas continued to stare into space while Walther laid out princely peacock blue ballroom attire.

"It is a pity your father could not be here tonight," continued Walther conversationally. "I'm sure he would like Lady Violet; she is a beautiful young lady."

"She is," agreed the Prince, without enthusiasm.

"And has a most congenial nature," continued Walther.

The Prince turned, folded his arms, crossed his legs, and leaned against the wall. "Why are we having this conversation, Walther? Have you heard from my father?"

Walther placed a folded sash on the bed, then turned, and folded his hands in a proper fashion. "Ahem, as a matter of fact, there was a small message this afternoon. You can appreciate that the King would rather be with you on your royal quest than having to stay at home looking after matters of state."

The Prince suppressed a grin. "Walther, we both know you are more than a simple valet. You handle all matters of protocol for Father and he trusts you to see to it that I toe the line and do not embarrass his Royal Stuffiness, so do strive to reach the point of the message."

"Yes. Ahem! The point is that his Royal Stuff—er—Majesty, the King has developed a bad case of impatience with your quest and suggests, delicately, that your possibly imagined peasant girl would not be expected to attend a Royal Ball."

The Prince strode up and down the chamber releasing his anger and frustration. When he felt he could speak reasonably, he faced his father's trusted Counsel.

"Walther, I mean no disrespect to Father, but do not be influenced by his suspicions and lack of faith in a son who has not always shown responsibilities to the crown. Trust me, Walther, please! I know she is not a peasant. She is a woman of nobility."

"You described her dress. You described her lame palfrey. Your description is not reassuring. Why would a noble woman dress as a peasant and ride a lame horse?"

"The horse was a pet, and she was on a mission. She was gentle, educated of speech, and refined, if you will. She was delicate. I know I am right."

"But you have worn out five pairs of shoes attending balls and discovered no—ahem!—'Fairy Princess.' Meanwhile, a beautiful young lady such as Lady Violet would make a most elegant and proper future queen, and your father..."

"Walther!" the Prince interrupted and, placing a hand on his Counsel's shoulder, looked him straight in the eye. "Lady Violet is lovely, amiable, and honest. She has made it quite clear to me that she loves Lucien. There is no question. She and I would be an unsuitable match."

"Then why are you putting on such a display of cordiality? The two of you seem to be most compatible."

Nicholas grinned and tossed his hair. "A little subterfuge. Violet tells me her mother is ambitious and though she was once quite satisfied with Lucien as a suitor, she decided a royal prince would be a superior match. Violet and I are merely posing until after the Ball. Then I shall depart without proposing marriage and her chagrined mama will be relieved and grateful that Lucien has remained faithful. Violet tells me her mother is quite capable of ugly scenes. This will save them embarrassment in front of their peers."

"Will this not be embarrassing for Violet—to be rejected?"

"Violet assures me it is not an issue. So, do I have your support in this charade?"

"Certainly, my Lord, but what of your quest?"

"Other guests are invited. There is always a chance that she will show up tonight," grinned Nicholas. "Now! Take on the role of Valet and help me prepare for the Ball." He turned away.

Behind his back, Walther shook his head. "Fat chance of that!"

Chapter 44

TREACHERY DEBUTS

A self-satisfied smirk seemed permanently etched on the Duchess's face as she surveyed the Great Hall. From the floral wreaths and garlands of green to the appetizing smells, everything was meticulously in order. The upper gallery was agog with onlookers and the feasting tables that lined the sides of the hall were full of well-dressed eager guests. The Duchess had planned for music and refreshment to continue all evening, simultaneously, with entertainment available at the clap of her hands.

The head table's seating arrangement had been slightly altered against her wishes, but she chose to overlook the small shift because she was so confident of her success. Thus, to her husband's right sat the Marquise Isabella, then Sir Frederick, then an empty seat for the Wizard—at Gregori's request. The Wizard had not yet arrived. Perhaps with any luck he would not show. Last on that side sat the amiable Marquis Arthur. To her own left sat the Prince who was contentedly chatting with Violet to his left. To her left sat Lucien, who had traded places with his father, and last sat Prudence, who had made no protest when she saw there was no place set for Verity, but was rather solemn.

The Duchess grinned. The receiving line had proceeded without alarm. The neighbouring nobility was eager to meet Prince Nicholas and introduce him to their eligible daughters. There was certainly no competition from those pale-faced, meek, and ugly waifs. The Prince had been most patient and polite and he looked eagerly up the line in anticipation. Darcus had reported a rumour to her that the Prince was looking for a mysterious lady he had once met, but whose identity he did not know. She shrugged. It hardly mattered now. He and Violet were deep in conversation, and Lucien just sat there impassively.

What a meek toad Lucien is. I wonder if I could pair him off with Verity, the Duchess thought. She became aware that Gregori was laughing at something Isabella had said. This would not do.

"Gregori!" she whispered sharply.

He turned toward her, still smiling. "Yes, dear?"

"Do not neglect your wife. It is unseemly."

"Sorry, my dear, but you seemed lost in thought and I cannot ignore our guests."

At that moment, Violet laughed out loud. The Duchess frowned at her behaviour. Both young men were turned toward her daughter, obviously in mid-tale. Rather than give Lucien any of her daughter's attention, the Duchess signalled the musicians for a sprightly tune, and in a moment, the Prince and Violet were up and dancing.

The Duchess relaxed and turned to her husband. "What is so captivating about Isabella, my dear?"

Gregori said, "She tells amusing stories about people she knows."

"She is a gossip," snapped the Duchess. "I hardly think that worthy of your attention."

"No, my dear, her stories are harmless—without malice. I think you should..." The Duke stopped, as a hush fell over the room. The music faded as the musicians strained to look over the edge of the gallery. All eyes were on the entrance to the Great Hall where two elegant strangers appeared. The elderly gentleman had a raven on his shoulder. He held the delicate hand of a beautiful fair-haired young woman dressed in sky blue silk. They paused at the top of the steps into the Great Hall.

"It is the Wizard," said the Duchess under her breath. "But who...?"

The Prince and Violet had stopped dancing. By the look on his face, he was spellbound, but he wasn't looking at Violet. Violet was smiling. Lucien was on his feet and moving rapidly across the hall to her. The Prince murmured something to Violet, kissed her hand courteously, and placed it firmly in Lucien's. He then moved rapidly toward the young woman in blue. He caught her free hand, kissed it gently, and kneeled before her. The room and all the people disappeared as Verity looked into the eyes of her love. She couldn't credit that he was actually here at the Ball, holding her hand, and dressed as royalty. Truth jarred her senses as she realized that the Prince and her huntsman were one and the same. Joy welled up in her breast, and she smiled.

The Prince rose and spoke to the Wizard, who gave his permission, and the Prince and the young woman descended the stairs to the ballroom floor. The musicians began playing again and the dancers resumed. All eyes were upon the Prince and his partner.

In awe, Gregori said softly, as if to himself, "She looks just like my mother!"

In the horror of recognition, Euphoria gasped, "Verity!"

Gregori smiled. "Yes, Verity. It seems your 'little toad' has become a Princess."

"But, how?" said the Duchess in shock. "Who is she?"

"I would venture to guess that Verity is my brother's daughter. As you pointed out, Euphoria, she looks nothing like Prudence and Frederick."

Prudence had risen from her seat upon the initial stunned surprise of Verity's entrance and changed appearance. She turned to meet Frederick's eyes across the table. They both observed the Duke and Duchess's shock. Prudence was by Frederick's side in a moment. She was frightened. But the Duchess smiled and moved her hand to the music as if she had not a care in the world.

Prudence took the empty seat between Arthur and Frederick. "I don't like it, Frederick; she will not accept defeat."

"Never you mind, my dear Prudence," interjected Arthur. "We are both ready, our swords are under the table and, besides, what can she do? There are too many people watching."

"Arthur's right," agreed Frederick. "We shall take Verity away immediately after the Ball. I'll arrange it." He stood and left through the kitchen doorway.

The Duchess noted his departure. A brief signal of her hand and Darcus appeared behind her. She whispered instructions to him and, when he left through the Salon, she clapped her hands merrily. Entertainers spilled into the room through the arch and began their merry antics. The dancers returned to their seats. The Prince and Verity sat to her left and Violet and Lucien took the end seats. Another place had been set at the other end of the table next to Arthur for the Wizard, who took his seat. Rothko flew up to the rafters and kept a beady eye on the events.

Arthur and Prudence welcomed the Wizard, turning their backs to the other end of the table. The Duke's favourite jugglers entertained him with their antics. Violet and Lucien were engrossed in each other. At that moment, a messenger approached the Prince, who quickly excused himself from Verity and left the Great Hall by the main entrance. The Duchess paid immediate attention to the jugglers as though she hadn't noticed the messenger. She laughed and waved her hands in pleasure. Her hand knocked over the Prince's wine glass and red liquid sprayed over Verity's blue dress. Verity gasped and brushed the spots with her hands. The Duchess moved swiftly.

"Come, dear Verity. I have something in the Salon that will clear up wine stains. The stains will disappear before the Prince returns, I promise you." She pulled Verity up and marched her unwilling but stunned body to the Salon door. Inside the Salon, Darcus was waiting.

The Duchess shoved Verity into his waiting arms and said, "Make haste, Darcus. I promised those spots would disappear before the Prince returns," she chuckled.

"Never fear, Milady, the deed is done."

Verity took a breath to scream, but Darcus stopped it with a hand covering her mouth before she had a chance. The Duchess was out the door and back in her seat admiring the jugglers with glee, before anyone but Rothko realized she had left the room.

$\mathfrak{G}$hapter 45

IMPRISONED

Verity struggled against Darcus's grip, but he was far stronger than her, and he kept her moving through the passageways. To resist him, she let her legs go slack as if she'd fainted, but he just lifted her off the ground and, with one arm around her waist and his hand gagging her mouth, he carried her swiftly away from all hope of rescue. She kicked within her long skirts. He laughed at her feeble attempts.

When they reached the stairwell to the Tower, Darcus roughly bound her arms and gagged her. He threw her over his shoulder and ran up the stairs as if she were a feather. At the Tower door, he didn't even bother to set her down. The elaborate crosshatch of nailed boards over the door was merely a ruse to make it seem that the door was nailed shut. He pulled it out on its hinges and opened the door with one hand. Closing both behind him, he took his time walking up the winding stair, feeling Verity's body with his free hand. When he set her down, he laughed as he looked into her blazing eyes.

"No one can hear you scream up here, my pretty little toad, so I shall remove the gag from your mouth."

He undid the cloth and pressed his lips against hers with rough, determined lust. He bent her back and pressed himself upon Verity's helpless body. Tears spilled down her face as despair overtook her. Verity eyed the Tower's window. She would rather be dead than be taken by Darcus. At last, Darcus let her go and pushed her to the floor.

"Pity that's all I can have for now. I am under orders to be sure no one disturbs the Tower. I will kill anyone who tries, but never fear, my lovely toad. I will return when the fuss is over and we will have our moment of passion together—like you could never imagine. For now, rest. Darcus is just outside the door protecting you from the nasty Princey. Tooraloo, sweet toad! I like your fair hair." He closed the door with a thud.

Verity lay on the cold stone spitting out the foul taste of Darcus. In no time, the floor was wet with tears. She struggled against her bonds. Luckily, Darcus had done a hasty job. She was sure she could find a way to free her arms, but what then? Firmly, she directed her thoughts to, *First thing's first.* And she tried to undo the knots behind her back.

Out in the hall, Darcus settled down to wait as ordered. He had an uneasy feeling he was not alone, so he looked around and lit another torch, placing it in a sconce. The flame reflected in a cocked black eye above him where he never thought to look. Darcus walked to the corner and looked down the passage, and then checked the stairs. No one. He returned to the entry steps to the Tower and sat down. After a while, he removed a leather flask from his jerkin and had a drink. Time passed slowly; the silence was complete. He settled himself more comfortably and dozed. A silent black shadow swooped down from the rafter, and flew down the stairs and out, unseen by Darcus.

Verity couldn't reach the knot. She relaxed her wrists and pulled with her fingers to move it to the front of her hands. She knew it would take time and she put all her concentration on the task behind her back.

Chapter 46

LIES

In the Great Hall, Violet's eyes focused as her father caught a juggler's ball and threw it back to him. She saw immediately that Verity and the Prince were out of their seats and, in fact, missing from the room.

"Where is Verity, Mother?"

The Duchess laughed again at the jugglers' tricks. She looked over her shoulder. "Verity?" she echoed vaguely. "Oh, she spilled something on her dress and went to cleanse it."

"And Prince Nicholas?" pursued Violet.

The Duchess looked vaguely unconcerned, and then gave a sly and leering look. "I expect he went to help her. They did rather like each other, didn't they?" and she turned back to a dancing monkey and laughed at his antics.

Violet looked around the room. No one seemed concerned. Lucien drew her attention to a magician flashing sparks from his hands, and she dismissed her concern for the moment. An exotic dancer from the East had the Wizard's head draped in filmy scarves. He pulled them away and tried to look around, but she held his face still, and swayed to the rhythm of an odd instrument he had never seen before. Prudence was listening to Arthur's reassurances that there was no imminent danger, and that everything was under control. But she kept her eye on the door to the Scullery where Frederick had gone. Isabella was alone and undistracted. Although she was short, she caught glimpses of empty space beyond the Duke and Duchess who were both tall and moving around, blocking her view. Isabella arose, and taking a quick peek, went to Prudence.

"Verity and the Prince have left," she announced quietly.

"Together?" asked Prudence.

"I assume so," answered Isabella.

"Sit by me," Prudence suggested. "Frederick has gone to make arrangements to take Verity out of here as soon as the Ball is over."

"That's wise," agreed Isabella.

Prince Nicholas returned. He approached Violet.

"Where is Verity?"

Violet assured him, "She has spilled a little wine on her dress. She will return in a moment." She smiled.

The Prince sat down and waited. He thought about the messenger—obviously nervous—and the bogus message, "There is news with Walther of your Father the King."

Nicholas, alarmed, had wondered at the lateness of the hour. Such a message after dark meant urgency, but Walther had been dozing in his chamber and knew of no such message.

Nicholas reached for his wine cup, now replenished, and drank deeply. Beside him, the Duchess smiled slyly and, biding for more time, introduced a subject concerning the royal court. She engaged him in conversation. At length, the entertainment ran its course and soothing music accompanied more food. Still, Verity did not return.

Prudence inquired of Violet and was told that Verity had spilled wine on her dress and had gone to remove it. It took a full two minutes before Prudence marched up to the Duchess and demanded to know where Verity was. The Duchess placated and wheedled, feigned ignorance, and then gave a great sigh and stated quietly, but firmly, that, after the Prince had left the room, Verity had vehemently stated that she could not tolerate such rudeness and had told the Duchess that she never wanted to see him again. The Prince's face went white. He looked at the Duchess in horror.

She raised her hand in a helpless gesture. "I tried to reason with her, but she said there was no point in trying to change her mind. She was leaving and she hoped to never see royalty again."

"Leaving? To where?" whispered Prudence, pale-faced. Frederick returned and stood behind her.

The Duchess smiled, "She said something about Florence. She said if her mother could do it so could she. What could I do? She's your daughter!"

Prudence fainted against Frederick, who nodded to the Prince. Nicholas summoned his Counsel Walther and disappeared from the Ballroom. Arthur and his Valet Mortimer left right behind them.

Lucien kissed Violet and said, "Make sure you don't disappear, my sweet." Then he followed his father.

The search had begun!

Chapter 47

THE TRUTH

Verity turned to her other side and rested her arm, which was numb from her weight. The pearl necklace shifted as she turned, and dropped to the other side of her neck. It reminded her of the Wizard's words: "You can't think as clearly when you cry."

She faced the window and patiently began again to loosen her bonds. Scratch. The slight sound made her look up. A shadow blocked the strong moonlight streaming in the window.

"Rothko! Oh, Rothko! Help me, please!"

The black bird hopped tidily down and peered carefully at the knot. He picked a spot and pulled with his strong beak. He pulled and pulled. It was tight. He hopped around to the other side and looked again. He picked another spot and pulled. He wiggled it from side to side and pulled again. It gave! Verity kept her hands still as he worked. At last, it loosened. Verity felt it free her right wrist. She pulled her hand free and sat up. Numbing pain shot up her arms, and she rubbed them vigorously.

Then she reached out and stroked Rothko, who cocked his head and trilled, "Cooooo."

"Thank you, dear friend. Now tell me. What do I do next?"

"Annalynn! Annalynn will tell." Rothko ruffled his feathers and waddled along the wall. "Let me see. Let me see," he repeated to himself, stopping now and then to look with one eye at the wall.

A dim memory wavered on the edge of Verity's mind. She remembered crawling along a curved wall of stone, and... there was a bird... a black, wonderful bird. Verity's heart raced in excitement. She pulled her skirts out of the way and crawled along the wall, searching it with her fingers. Images of Prudence floated into her mind... and a feather. Her hands grew more frantic and then... there was the lever! She pressed. The wall opened. Rothko stood where he had stopped right in front of the secret compartment. He gave a small squawk.

Verity grinned at him. "So, you were here first, I know. Let's see what we have." She put her hand in and pulled out a feather, glossy and black. "So you've been here before, you rogue," she said affectionately. Rothko nodded his head up and down vigorously.

Verity reached in again with two hands. She pulled out an old writing box. She opened it eagerly. Inside were scrolls of parchment with faint writing. She couldn't read it even in the strong light of the full moon. The white goose feathers sat at the front. Memories of a feather stroking her cheek made her put the scrolls tidily back in the box. She returned to the secret hole in the wall.

"I remember there was something more, but I left it there." She reached in once again to the touch of leather and pulled a large heavy pouch out of its hiding place. She opened the top and pulled out a coin. In the moonlight, the gold glistened. The pouch was full of gold coins. She wondered whose the fortune was. Perhaps the scrolls of parchment would tell her.

"Think," she told herself and looked around the Tower. It was furnished sparsely with one chair and one writing table. She pulled the chair to the writing table and explored the compartments at the back. In a small drawer, she found a lighting device and a candleholder, but there were no candles. Rothko perched on top of the desk, watching her intently.

"Rothko," she petted the bird, "I need a candle. Can you...?" The bird's wings spread and he flew out the window.

Verity sat in the chair and thought as hard as she could. The moon had shifted and the room grew dimmer. She remembered being in the Tower with her mother and she remembered the hole in the wall, but the entry door down the stairs did not fit her recollection. Somehow, it was wrong.

The hour was late and her eyes grew heavy. Rothko was taking a long time. She thought about her mother. A faint glow illuminated the stones in the Tower wall. It grew and brightened. Suddenly, Verity was awake. Her heart pounded, but she was not frightened. She peered at the light and concentrated. Gradually, a woman appeared with fair hair tumbling across her shoulders. She beckoned to Verity, inviting her attention and then, turning to the wall, pointed to a wall sconce. The wall opened as if it were a door. The light flickered and faded. In the dim light, Verity looked around the Tower wall. Round and round it went. There was no wall sconce, and except for the opening to the stairwell—which led to Darcus—there was no other door to the Tower. Verity shivered.

Rothko squawked from the window and leaped to the desk. In his beak was a taper. Rapidly, Verity lit the candle and began to read.

"My arms held one son, and then the other, before my husband enclosed me in his love, and then they were off to do battle. I ached with fear, but left my chamber to keep vigil in the Tower and there in time Rothko told me."

Verity looked up at Rothko, whose head was cocked as he watched her intently. She patted him gently and continued to read.

"The rasps and clanks of a hundred swords swirled the morning mist as the battle between the knights of the green plume and the knights of the red plume grew fierce." Verity suddenly looked up again and repeated aloud, "'...left my chamber to keep vigil in the Tower...' That's where the sconce is and the second entrance. Perhaps I can escape Darcus if I hurry before the Duchess returns."

She scanned down the written words: "...her golden curls reflect the sunlight in the garden. Prudence, her nurse, takes the best care of little Sunshine. Honore loved her daughter, too. I wish she had survived the plague. Stephen is so lost without Honore. It is no wonder, in his grief, that he calls his daughter 'Sunshine' instead of her given name, 'Verity.' I fear the Black Death. Now,

Stephen looks pale. Please God, spare our little Sunshine." The catch in Verity's throat broke out in a sob. She caught her breath and kept reading. "I shall keep Honore's dowry hidden for her child and my spirit shall not rest until her child knows the truth."

Verity could wait no longer. She replaced the manuscript and the box as well as the pouch of gold. Then she hesitated and removed one coin, hiding it in her dress.

Closing the wall, she spoke softly to the bird, "I must leave the Tower before the Duchess comes to kill me or imprison me forever. Come, Rothko."

Grasping the candlestick, Verity tiptoed down the staircase with Rothko on her shoulder. Near the bottom of the stairs by the door, Verity faced the left wall. Rothko's head bobbed up and down, and then stopped with his beak pushed forward. Verity silently explored the area indicated and found the catch. The wall moved silently inward. Verity's heart pounded. Would anyone be in the Duchess's chamber?

She slipped through and glanced around at the bed, wardrobe, and enormous mirror in the corner. The wall closed behind her. She went to the door and opened it a crack. Faintly, she could hear snoring. Darcus! She must get out now. She looked back at the room. There on a chair was a discarded cloak. She coaxed Rothko off her shoulder and threw the black garment over herself, pulling up the hood to cover her fair hair. Rothko reperched himself as Verity dowsed the candle and they left the chamber in darkness.

In the passage, Darcus continued to snore. Verity crept to the corner. Maiden and bird peeked around the corner at the sleeping Darcus. After a moment, and as silent as shades, the two slipped past and descended the stairwell.

Chapter 48

THE SEARCH

Just inside the castle door, Frederick controlled the hub of operations. So far, the search had yielded no sign of Verity. Prudence was soon by his side.

"Isabella and I have gathered the maids. They will check all the bedchambers carrying fresh linens as a pretext, and will report to Isabella any rooms they are unable to enter. Where are the others?"

Frederick laid a reassuring hand on her shoulder. "Bennefield and Mortimer are searching the Scullery. She could be tossed in the vegetable bins or locked in the larder. It shouldn't take them long, because if that's where she was taken, one of the servants would have seen something. Arthur and Garrod have gone to the stables, just in case Euphoria was speaking true. Garrod and the stable hands know every inch of the place, so they can soon determine if Verity's horse or any cart has left."

"And Prince Nicholas?" asked Prudence.

"The Prince and Lucien have gone to the dungeons. His valet, Walther, went as well. He is armed and acts with authority. Just between you and me, I think there's more to him than meets the eye. They have decided to free all the poor souls down there."

Prudence shivered, "I pray she is not there."

Frederick nodded, "I share your horror."

Prudence stiffened. "Could she be in the Tower?"

Frederick shook his head. "No, I understand the door to it has been nailed shut for a long time. It seems a ghost in the Tower frightened Euphoria and she had it boarded up many years ago before we left. They wouldn't have had time to open it."

"But that's not the only entrance!"

"What did you say?"

Prudence looked frantic. "She must be there! The other entrance is in the Duchess's chamber. There is a secret lever by the left sconce. The wall opens onto the stairwell to the Tower room."

"I'll be sure to have the Prince check the Tower next."

"And where is the Wizard?" continued Prudence anxiously.

Frederick gestured toward the Great Hall. "The party continues. He's keeping an eye on the Duke and his witch of a wife. We can't have her free to wreak further havoc. Violet is there as well. Don't look so desolate, Prudence; we'll find Verity safe and sound."

Prudence grasped her husband's arm. Suddenly her eyes went wide with horror.

"Frederick, where is Darcus?"

His face broke in agony and Frederick gathered Prudence in his arms, holding her head against his shoulder.

He bent his head and whispered to her, "If that snake touches Sunshine, I swear to you and God, I will kill him!"

Tears blurred Prudence's eyes as she thought that at last he had remembered.

She faced her husband and quietly urged, "Go, Frederick. Verity must be in the Tower."

"I cannot leave you here alone, and someone has to be here when the others return with reports." He paused. "I know, I'll get the priest for now. The others shouldn't be long."

With a few strides, Frederick stepped into the Great Hall. Euphoria's eyes narrowed as she watched him walk to the priest and shake him, but the priest was sleeping the sleep of the dead, and Frederick returned to the front hallway. Behind him, the Duchess smirked. For the last course, the subtlety, she had arranged for a gentle sleeping potion to be added to the wine. The pastry cook had been well trained by her harsh demands and the pastry-made fire-breathing dragon had distracted everyone from the change of wine. The fire had been Euphoria's own creation simply by stuffing the dragon's open mouth with camphor-soaked material.

Euphoria looked around at the sprawling guests. For people who had overeaten, the sleeping potion had been very effective. Even the Wizard and Violet were dozing peacefully, but the others from the head table had left before enjoying the effects of her clever and soporific potion. The Duchess tasted the last of her sweetmeat and licked her fingers. A sip of her own chaste wine made her smile. It was an excellent port, she thought, and she gazed at her hands clad in golden ruby rings with sweet contentment.

As he rejoined Prudence in the hallway, Frederick said, "Everyone, including the priest, is drugged. I pray the Wizard is not. I saw his foot move under the table. We'll have to wait. One of our searchers will return anon and I'll go search the Tower."

A moment later, Arthur and Garrod returned from the stables.

Arthur said, "All is quiet. Dolphus is still there munching his oats and the stable hands swear no carts or horses have left tonight. Garrod made a good search of the place while I made inquiries. I checked her palfrey myself. She is not there and I'm fairly certain she hasn't been there tonight."

"The Tower, Frederick!" insisted Prudence.

"Yes, my dear. Arthur, Prudence has suggested the Tower be checked again. Would you stay with her while I have a look?"

"You know I will. Take Garrod with you."

"No need, Arthur—one person makes less sound."

Frederick handed his dagger to Prudence. Hand on hilt, Frederick turned to the stairs, but stopped when he heard his name.

"Sir Frederick! Stay!"

Prince Nicholas ran down the hall with Lucien a few steps behind him. Returned from the dungeons, the young men looked as though they had seen the horrors of hell. Eyes wide, mouths agape, both trembled. Arthur steadied his son.

Lucien babbled, "...skeletons... moved..." and broke into tears.

Frederick put an arm around the Prince who seemed too stunned to speak.

Prudence looked into the young man's face and asked in a gentle but shaky voice, "Verity?"

Tears streaming down his face, Nicholas answered softly, "No, Milady. Thanks be to God, my Fairy Princess was not there!"

Prudence released a sob of relief.

Gradually, the Prince recovered himself and took a deep breath. "It was the prisoners. Not fed. Only water piped in from the lake. Not even a jailor. They were left to starve to death. Some were dead and then some moved." He shuddered again. "Walther told us to report to you and he would release the ones who are still alive."

Frederick turned to Prudence. "The Tower it must be. I will return." He ran for the stairwell.

Prudence took Nicholas's hand and he asked, "Is there no word?"

Mutely, Prudence shook her head, but gave a weak smile. "At least we know where she is not!" The four stood in a circle and looked at the floor in solemn silence, wondering where the truth lay.

Chapter 49

THE DUCHESS IN ACTION

Inside the Great Hall, the Duke and Duchess appeared to be rather drunk, and Violet, with her head propped on her arm, was asleep. After abstaining from his wine, the Wizard had observed Euphoria clumsily pouring a dose of blue potion from her ring into his goblet. He had pretended to drink from it, until she turned her attention to her daughter, and then he poured it out under the table. When Violet's head had dropped and she slept, he feigned the same reaction and pretended to sleep, assuming that the Duchess had given them both the same potion. After a while, he observed Frederick trying to rouse the priest and moved his foot to alert his friend that he was under no spell of the Duchess.

Soon afterward he heard, "Come, Gregori! They are both asleep. We have to dispose of Verity!"

The Duke protested blearily. "Why? The child has done nothing wrong and, heh, heh, heh, I think the Prince likes her!"

"Exactly!" said the Duchess, as she pulled him to his feet. "And we have to save him for our Violet. Come, Gregori, come!" Two of her long fingernails broke as she tugged at her reluctant husband.

The Duke hung back and paused by his sleeping daughter. He patted her head.

"Have a nice nap, little flower."

A sigh of exasperation came from the Duchess. "Come, Gregori!" She pulled him toward the Salon. A lock of her hair came loose and dangled grey and untidy down the side of her face.

"Can I stay and have a nap too? See, everyone's having a nap."

He waved his hand to indicate the hall and, in fact, many people were asleep from too much wine. The Duchess glanced back at the Wizard, asleep at the table.

"Good for them. Come, Gregori!" She pushed and pulled him toward the door.

As soon as the door closed behind them, the Wizard took rapid steps after them. Of course, the door was now locked, but that was not a problem for him. He opened it as the other door out of the Salon was closing. He slipped through the door. He released his dark cloak, which was fastened on his shoulder and hung down his back. He threw it over himself and entered the passage. He was nearly invisible in the dark. The only part of him that gleamed was the glint in his eye.

Pulling her husband, sometimes pushing, the Duchess finally achieved her Bedchamber. Darcus couldn't help but hear them as they approached, and helped her the rest of the way. While he laid the Duke on the bed, she prepared a potion for her husband. Her hair fell out of its pins and draggled down on one side.

Darcus held the Duke as she poured a potion down his drunken throat. "Are you putting him to sleep or killing him?"

"Don't be an ass, Darcus. I may need him later. I'm waking him up. Let him lie there and recover while we put Verity to sleep permanently."

"Why are you going to kill her? You promised I could have her first!"

"Don't whine, Darcus, there isn't time for that. We'll dump her out of the Tower. When she hits the rocks below, she should sleep for a few million years. Come! We don't have much time before Gregori wakens."

They rushed out of the chamber and through the passage to the main Tower door. Darcus held open the nailed slat screen while the Duchess unlocked the door. They hurried up the steps with a torch.

The Tower was empty.

"Perhaps she killed herself," cried Darcus as he rushed to the window. But he could not see straight down because the window-sill was too high.

The Duchess snarled, "She could not have done that, Darcus; the window ledge is too high and the chair is not under it. She must have escaped under your oh-so-watchful eye." She spun around and walked out.

Darcus followed closely behind her. He did not want to be left alone in the haunted Tower.

ℭhapter 50

THE PARTY'S OVER

Below them in the passage, the soft swish of steps could be heard from the stairwell. Sir Frederick emerged looking cautiously around the hallway and into the cul-de-sac where the Tower entrance lay wide open—Frederick could see the cleverly rigged latticed covering hanging on its hinges—and the sound of voices arguing drifted down.

"Hssst!"

Frederick drew his sword and shrank back close to the wall of the stairwell.

"Hssst! Frederick!" came a whisper from the passage to his right.

Frederick ran lightly toward the whispered summons. The Wizard drew him into the doorway of Violet's room and whispered in his ear.

"The Duke is waking in their chamber, and Euphoria and Darcus have found the Tower empty—much to their chagrin!" He chuckled. "It seems Verity has flown the coop and has left them most puzzled. Shh... here they come."

Arguing noisily, the Duchess and Darcus left the Tower cul-de-sac and turned the corner to her Bedchamber. After a few minutes, Euphoria had roused her husband, and the three walked down the passage and continued past the main stairwell, still arguing. Two silent shadows watched from their hiding place, smiling grimly. Down in the main hallway, the minutes passed slowly as the little group waited. So far, there had been no word from Bennefield and Mortimer who had gone to the Scullery. Garrod had left to join them, because he knew the Scullery so well. Lucien and Nicholas paced.

Prudence wandered aimlessly and tried to keep breathing. She heard a sound from the stairs. Frederick and the Wizard appeared.

"Was she there?" Prudence asked anxiously.

"No," said Frederick.

"But she had been there," continued the Wizard. "Our clever little sprite evidently escaped right under the nose of the despicable Darcus."

Prince Nicholas chuckled as Prudence wailed, "But where is she now?"

She sucked in a gasp as she looked past the men to see two cloaked and hooded figures on the stairs. A black-winged shadow floated close behind.

The short figure, Pagley, complained sharply, "She scared me to death, but here she is!"

Verity removed her hood and Prudence threw her arms around her daughter in relief, assuring herself that this was no apparition.

Nicholas grasped Verity's two hands in his and asked, "Where have you been?"

"In Grandmother's Tower, where I learned the truth. The Duchess put me there under the guard of Darcus."

"Did he hurt you?" queried the Prince and Frederick in unison.

"No, I'm fine!" assured Verity, suddenly feeling shy under the Prince's intense gaze. She grinned at the Prince, who impulsively stepped forward and took her in his arms. Prudence smiled and reached for Frederick's hand. There was a moment of bliss and relief for all.

Finally, Bennefield and Walther arrived. The big bear-like giant looked shaken.

Walther explained, "The prisoners made directly for the Scullery; their first need was food."

"Skeletons!" whispered Bennefield.

Walther continued, "We tried to help, but now the kitchen staff are coping with Mortimer and Garrod's assistance."

"Pagley, inform the Marquise of our progress, and tell her we shall be in the Great Hall. Come, Frederick, let us deal with the Duchess," ordered Prudence, and she walked toward the Great Hall with everyone at her heels.

Their entrance was an anticlimax: the Duchess was not there and everyone in the Hall was asleep. The party was definitely over.

"She will probably return here by the back stairs," ventured the Wizard.

"We shall wait," declared Prudence and took Verity's hand. "Tell me dear, what truth did you learn in the Tower?"

Verity grinned. "I learned you used to call me 'Sunshine' just as my Father had done. You were my nursemaid. My Mother had died. Grandmother wrote it down and I read it."

Prudence remembered the scrolls very well. "We must get you out of here, my darling Verity. Now that the truth is known, you are in grave danger."

They looked soberly at each other, when suddenly a grim, raspy voice sounded behind them.

"Not so fast, you pin in my side," the Duchess and Darcus had entered the Great Hall from the Scullery. "I should have killed you years ago, Prudence, but I underestimated you. I don't make mistakes twice. Kill her, Darcus. Kill them all."

Darcus pulled his sword, rushing toward Prudence. Frederick stepped up to block him and their swords met with a loud clang in the echoing room.

Violet woke up with a start and watched in horror. She saw her mother, hair streaked with grey and in her snagged purple dress, and her father quite greyed as well. There was Verity, now fair-haired with Nicholas standing in front of her, one hand protecting her, one hand grasping a sword at the ready. Sir Frederick and Darcus were matching swords. Violet rose and rushed out into the room. Lucien caught her and held her back. The Wizard restrained Prudence.

After several noisy parries, Frederick and Darcus locked swords, face to face. "Did you molest her?"

Darcus grinned. "Naturally," he crowed.

Frederick broke the lock and stepped back. Darcus waggled his sword and laughed at his own lie. Frederick lunged forward and Darcus backed away frantically. His sudden panicked leap backward impaled him on the Prince's sword. Darcus laughed no more. Nicholas let go of the hilt and pulled Verity to his chest, so that she would not see, but she had seen enough.

"Darcus! My son!" cried the Duchess and fell forward onto him.

The Duke's knees buckled as he went into shock at his wife's words. Arthur helped him to a seat. The Duchess rose with Darcus's dagger in her hand. She shouted for guards to take away Sir Frederick for murder but, against her orders, they had sampled the wine and were all asleep. She then staggered forward, tripping on her dress.

"It was you all along," she said to Prudence in a low, menacing voice. "You knew the truth and kept the secret."

She raised the dagger as she took another step.

"That's enough, Euphoria!" shouted the Wizard from behind her.

Euphoria spun around and threw the dagger at the Wizard's heart. Rothko was already in flight. He swerved and intercepted the dagger enough to slap it to the floor with a useless clatter.

"Your magic days are over, Euphoria," boomed the Wizard. "Give up now and enjoy some days of peace."

"We'll see about that," defied the Duchess. "I challenge you to a duel, Wizard. If you are not too frightened to take on a Wicca!"

The Duchess extracted a small wineskin from a secret pocket in her dress. She eagerly gulped it down; red trickles, like blood, spilled down her chin. She wiped her mouth with her hand. The rouge on her lips and the potion smeared all over her face and hands.

"That won't do you any good, Euphoria. The magic is gone. Your flowers are destroyed. The potion you drink is a substitute I made."

The Duchess looked at Verity. "You went for my flowers," she accused.

Verity shook her head. "They were dead when I got there. They were lost in a powdered fog."

Euphoria turned to her husband, "Gregori, you filled my chest with powder."

Gregori shook his head. "No, Euphoria, I did not."

"It was I who filled your chest with useless powder," said the Wizard. "So you are useless as well."

"But I drank it... it was powerful... I don't understand..."

"Only a little dizziness from my potion and your own imagination," countered the Wizard.

Euphoria turned away. Her hair fell down on the other side of her head as she brushed it with her hand. The dark colour from her hair streamed down with her sweat and stained her dress. She rubbed her eyes as if she couldn't see straight. The dark makeup from the East smudged her eye sockets. All the defiance and all the fight went out of her body in a sigh and she walked away, stooped and old. Verity remembered the old woman she had seen picking the flowers that day so long ago. Her beauty had only been paint and illusion.

There was a moment of stunned silence.

The Wizard raised his arm. Rothko swooped over and landed on his shoulder. "I could use a goblet of fresh wine, old friend. How about you?"

Rothko cocked his head, "Fresh fish? Cheese? Sweetmeats?" Rothko was a hungry bird. Together, they left for the kitchen.

Frederick and Arthur began rousing the guests who, by now, were waking from the commotion. Quickly, the hall was cleared of the sleeping and the dead.

The priest, Prudence, and a now-awakened Kailan entered the Salon and began to plan its restoration as the castle's Chapel. Isabella wandered in after them, smiling, as she saw Lucien and Violet embrace. *They will soon have need of a Chapel,* she thought.

The Duke took Verity's hands in his. "I have known about you for some time, dear niece, but I did not have the least idea how to stand up to my wife."

"But you protected me from Darcus," Verity replied, "and for that I am grateful."

"Did he hurt you?" asked the Duke.

"Only an ugly kiss," replied Verity. "He was too afraid of the Duchess to do more."

"His own mother," said the Duke.

"Yes, Uncle," said Verity.

"Thank God he did no more!" said Frederick, who had heard every word.

"Yes, thank God," said Gregori, who smiled at Frederick—his brother's best friend. Frederick smiled back.

"Thank God," echoed Nicholas, who once again collected Verity in his arms. Verity said no more. She was being thoroughly kissed right before her father's gaze, but Frederick was not about to object.

Violet turned to Lucien and they happily followed suit. Nodding at Frederick, Gregori was beginning to feel a sense of optimism.

Chapter 51

MONSTER

The Wizard returned, leading Mortimer who looked shaken. Arthur looked up at his Valet, "Mortimer, has something happened?"

Mortimer was mute as he nodded.

The Wizard spoke, "It's the Duchess. She came down the back stairwell and was spotted by the released prisoners. Some of them attacked her."

Violet cried out and covered her face.

The Wizard shook his head and said, "I'm sorry, Violet, but your mother is possessed and desperate. She was armed and lashed out at her attackers. She wounded two and killed one—her former hairdresser. Agatha told us that the woman had been imprisoned for pulling your mother's hair."

Violet faltered, "Where is she now?"

The Wizard answered quietly, "The Duchess has left the castle and was last seen riding toward the woods. She is probably heading for her precious flowers."

Slowly, the group absorbed the new information.

Frederick asked, "And what of the wounded?"

The Wizard said, "Garrod is now addressing their needs and has Agatha tending to their wounds. He has become quite a capable young man, Frederick, but I venture to say that you know that already."

"Come, Lucien," ordered the Prince. "We must not let the pitiful woman harm herself or anyone else." Bennefield, Frederick, and Walther followed them.

For a moment, the Duke watched Violet standing alone as dry sobs shook her body. He went to his daughter and took her in his arms until she quietened.

Then, he gently kissed her on the forehead and said, "It's alright, little flower, I love you. I'm going to your mother now—she needs me." Resignedly, he turned and left the Great Hall after the other men.

Verity put an arm around Violet and led her to the dais for some wine and a sturdy chair. Isabella kindly suggested she could take Violet to bed for a little rest, but Violet shook her head and held tightly to Verity, who thought, *It's going to be a long night.*

In the stables, the groomsmen saddled the steeds.

Frederick nodded to Gregori. "Thank you for coming."

The Duke replied quietly, "It is the least I can do. I know where the flowers are—were grown. The Wizard claims they are destroyed. I hope so, but Euphoria will fall apart when she sees that. I have no idea how she will react. I was despondent when I stopped using the flowers' power, but she has depended on it since childhood."

"Why did you stop?" asked Frederick.

"Because I knew Violet would need me... not that I've been much help."

"It's not too late for you and your daughter to make amends." Frederick mounted his steed. "Come. Let us see if there is anything left to save in the swamp."

It was a short ride in the predawn light to the meadow where the seven horsemen stopped just above the undulating white cloud.

"We dare not take our horses where we cannot see," declared the Prince.

He dismounted and they all followed the wisdom of his words. The black mare and the Duchess were nowhere in sight. The Duke stepped into the swirling mist and disappeared. One by one, the others followed, leaving Walther to assure the safety of the horses.

Gregori called softly, "Euphoria, Fori, it's time to come home now."

Frederick stumbled, kicking up some swamp water before he regained his footing.

"Stay to the high grass. Don't step on anything flat!" he warned the others.

They moved ahead following the dark shadow of the Duke. A sharp gasp was all the warning they had, as they advanced to the most mournful and unnerving sight. Covered in white powder, the Duchess was laying half in the swamp and half on solid ground. The Duke was on his knees beside her, brushing off the white powder. Euphoria was still breathing and out of her open mouth poured a dense, almost solid, stream of white. The ether rose and took form. It looked like Euphoria, but it was not. It looked solid, yet not.

Gregori was rubbing her hands. "Wake up, Fori. Stop this monster! You don't need it any more."

Low pitched and guttural, a voice spoke to him from the ether. "Useless, feeble husband—do shut up! She is no more! I, and only I, am supreme."

A red glow grew stronger around the form. Black eyes gleamed with flashes of red. It was so monstrously large that it made Bennefield look like a boy. However, with stout heart, he ran forward and thrust his sword with all his strength into the centre of the monster. There being no substance to the monster, Bennefield fell forward into the swamp. Lucien and Nicholas pulled him out. Frederick approached the entity. With a mighty swing, he cut the monster in half but, again with no substance to the monstrosity, he continued to spin and lost his footing and fell.

Lucien pulled him aside as the monster laughed in ridicule. "Giants and Barons are no threat to me. Go and tend your worn-out castles and puny wives."

Lucien quietly made his way to the back of the monstrous form to examine it. It looked solid, yet floated in the air. The glowing red substance spun around the monster, whispering shrilly. He could almost imagine the demons within. He thrust his dagger tentatively into the red mist. The hilt grew red hot and he dropped the weapon into the swamp. Carefully, he made his way back to the others. Nicholas had his sword in hand. He looked perplexed but willing.

Lucien said, "Wait, friend, I have an idea. Just let it sit there feeding on its own arrogance. I'll be back in a moment." The white fog swallowed him up.

Out in the meadow, Lucien conferred with Walther who mounted his horse and took off like a bolt of lightning. Lucien opened his pannier and removed a mirror. It had never given him any benefit. His hair was too unruly, but he carried it to please his mother. He returned to the swamp and spoke quietly to Nicholas. The Prince took the mirror and hid it in his tunic. With sword in hand, he approached the apparition.

The monster stilled. "You are my nemesis," it hissed. "It is you who have brought me down. It was your love that gave Verity the strength to destroy my flowers. You are the cause, and now you must die!"

The form turned fiery red and lashed out at the Prince who fought bravely. She spewed out limb after limb of fire. The whole swamp glowed with the fury of their battle.

Closer and closer came the face with eyes of lightning. "I shall smite thee, you puny persistent peacock of a prince!"

A fiery pain in his arm made the Prince stagger to the side. His legs buckled; he went down on one knee. The monster bore down with flaming mouth and flashing eyes. Nicholas dropped his sword and reached into his tunic. He held the mirror up to the descending face. As the monster's power reflected back into itself; its features blackened and disappeared. Nicholas rose and thrust the mirror into the swirling flames and, in a moment, all was quiet as the flames extinguished.

Through the white fog, Walther appeared, carrying full wineskins. Lucien grasped one and squirted it at the solid white form. It dissolved slowly. The others took wineskins and sprayed the liquid liberally over the whole area. The fog dissolved and the monster was gone.

With all his strength, Gregori tried to pull Euphoria out of the quicksand, but she cried out in pain, "Let me be!"

He took her hand and kissed her palm.

Euphoria looked up at her husband. "Gregori, can you forgive me?"

Choking on words, he nodded.

Euphoria closed her eyes and tears ran down her face. "Will Violet cry for me?"

"Yes," Gregori whispered. "She loves you and so do I."

Euphoria slipped further into the black watery muck. Gregori tried to hold onto her. Lucien gripped Gregori's body and held on. Euphoria stopped breathing.

Gregori whispered, "Euphoria?"

Her body slipped again. He tried desperately to hold on, but she slipped into the swamp and was gone. Gregori reached into the muck to pull her out, but there was nothing there. Lucien tried as well. Both kneeled on the bank, looking down at the shiny black surface that showed nothing but two faces of sadness and heartbreak.

Lucien put a hand on the Duke's shoulder. "She's gone, Milord. There is nothing more we can do."

Gregori whispered, "Gone, yes. Euphoria... gone. She died first, you know—before the quicksand took her—the quick and the dead. I loved her, you know..." His words trailed off.

"I understand," said Lucien. "I know what love is. Come, Milord, there is nothing more to do here and Violet needs you."

They turned. Arthur was standing behind them. With support from the two of them, Gregori walked back to the meadow. There, the injured Prince sat on the grass between Walther and Bennefield.

Walther said, "The swamp has cleared. Here they come. Now we must tend to your injuries, Nicholas."

Gregori heard Walther's words and saw the Prince's burns. The Duke stood tall and unsupported.

"Come," Gregori said to Nicholas, "I know where we can fix those burns. Can you ride?"

The Prince nodded. They mounted their horses and rode up the path to the pond. No one looked back.

Chapter 52

CONCLUSION

Violet cried. Her father gently told her the news from the swamp; he told her that her Mother's last thought was of her.

"She did love you, Violet. I promise you that. I love you, too." And he hugged her tightly.

After a while, Isabella guided Violet to her chamber. She gently tucked the daughter she could soon count as her own into bed. Isabella dozed in a chair at Violet's bedside; Lucien disturbed her so many times with inquiries about Violet that she finally found an extra blanket and pushed her son into another chair by the bed and told him to be quiet and let the poor girl sleep.

All that day, the castle was quiet. It was a peaceful quiet. There were no raised voices in anger or alarm. Under the calm was a current of activity. The murmur of voices swelled then faded as hated chores disappeared and the castle was lovingly cared for.

But the next morning, a loud voice echoed down the passages, "I cannot wait another moment. I have been patient long enough. After all my searching, hoping, despairing…"

Walther's murmur interrupted.

"No!" shouted the Prince, "Don't preach patience. I'm done with waiting!"

In the Great Hall, Prudence and Isabella exchanged a smile over cups of mead. The small breakfast group looked very content.

Prudence said, "I brought two wedding dresses from Florence."

The Duke said, "I helped the priest restore the Chapel."

Isabella said, "I have decorated the Chapel with flowers."

Frederick said, "Are the girls prepared?"

From the back passage came Lucien's voice. "Don't tell me to be patient, Father. I've waited long enough."

From the Chapel came two giggles.

Frederick said, "Never mind, I see they are prepared. Let us have a double ceremony tonight. I have never been one to procrastinate."

Prudence smiled. "That's part of your charm, dear."

That evening, the wedding guests gathered in the Great Hall. Soon, Verity and Violet, ablush with excitement, entered from the hall followed by Pagley and Fiametta, flushed with pride. All day, they had stitched, beaded, brushed, and braided until they had produced two beautiful brides dressed in creamy silk. Smiles of pride encircled the room.

The Duke stepped forward and asked if he might give Verity's hand in marriage as her closest relative.

Frederick was crestfallen. "But you are already giving Violet's hand in marriage!"

The Wizard spoke up, "If you don't mind, I think I will claim seniority, as Verity is my Great Granddaughter."

Frederick looked at Prudence who smiled and nodded her approval. He relaxed and took her arm. The priest emerged from the Chapel to greet the wedding party. Old Agatha led in the two mothers; the rest crowded into the Chapel.

As the Wizard put Verity's hand through his arm and patted it, Verity grinned, "I knew your mysterious past would catch up with you sooner or later, Sir Wizard!"

She squeezed his arm and they followed Gregori and Violet into the Chapel where Prince Nicholas and Sir Lucien now waited. The Chapel was filled to capacity. Rothko watched from his perch amid the flowers decorating a sconce.

The ceremony began.

Epilogue

Violet and Lucien chose to stay with her father, the Duke of Grenwoodle.

Prudence and Frederick returned to repair the von Balford estate.

Isabella and Arthur went home to the Cortelaide Castle to await grandchildren.

Verity and Nicholas travelled to the King's Castle, where more pomp and ceremony took place to celebrate the country's joy.

The Wizard spent the rest of his peaceful life with Rothko in their cottage in the woods. From time to time, visitors spoke of his talking to his daughter Annalynn, but they never saw her ghostly presence.

And as far as I know, they all lived happily ever after.

The End

This chronicle was written by Father Roth, Priest of Grenwoodle.

Glossary

"Above the salt"

Above the salt (or *below the salt*) are expressions that describe someone's rank or importance in medieval times. Salt was an expensive and treasured spice, and only higher ranking people had access to salt on the table during meals.

Armour

Protective clothing made of fabric, metal plates, or chain mail, designed to protect the wearer from the impact of weapons.

Armoury

A place where weapons (also known as "arms") are stored.

Bailey – courtyard

An outer wall of a castle, and/or a courtyard within a castle.

Brace

A pair of animals, typically birds or small mammals, killed in hunting, and often tied together.

Caravan

A group of people, often with pack animals, travelling together.

Chemise

A woman's loose-fitting undergarment, or a dress hanging straight from the shoulders.

Cotte

An outer garment worn by men and women during medieval times.

Curfew
A medieval regulation requiring people to extinguish fires at a fixed hour in the evening [from the Anglo-French 'coverfu' (cover fire)].

Curtsy
A formal greeting made by a woman or girl, made by bending the knees and lowering the body.

Debit
A record of a payment made.

Destrier
A warhorse; a large, strong horse ridden into battle.

Doublet
A close-fitting jacket, with or without sleeves, worn by men.

Draught
An air current in a confined space, such as a room or a chimney; or a dose of liquid medicine.

Drawbridge
A bridge, often over water, hinged at one end so that it may be raised and lowered to prevent passage and/or to allow ships to pass.

Falconer
A keeper or trainer of hawks, and/or a person who hunts with hawks.

Falconry
The breeding and training of hawks, and/or the sport of hunting with hawks.

Fortnight
A period of two weeks (from 'fourteen nights').

Garret
A room on the top floor or attic of a castle, often small and dismal.

Goshawk
A large, short-winged hawk.

Harridan
A bad-tempered woman.

Hennin
Cone-shaped headdress worn by noble women in the Middle Ages.

Jerkin
A sleeveless jacket.

Jousting
A 'joust' is a sporting event between two knights who fight with lances while on horseback.

Keep, the
A tower or stronghold with the castles of nobility during medieval times.

Knight
A man who served as an armoured soldier, on horseback, during medieval times.

Lackey
A servant.

Latin
The language of ancient Rome.

Lean-to
A shelter consisting of a sloped roof supported on one side by trees or posts and covered with canvas, branches, etc.

Liripipe
A hood with a lengthy tail that was wound around the neck like a scarf.

Lists in a jousting tournament, the
A fence of iron railings that enclosed an area for a jousting tournament.

Mead
An alcoholic drink of fermented honey and water.

Mews
A set of stables around an open yard or along a lane.

Minstrel
A medieval singer or musician, especially singing or reciting poetry.

Molest
Attack or interfere with a person, especially sexually; annoy or pester a person in a hostile or injurious way.

Mule
The offspring of a donkey and a horse, used to carry heavy loads.

Overseer
A person who supervises others, especially workers.

Palfrey
A gentle-natured horse for everyday riding, especially for women.

Pallet
A straw mattress or small, uncomfortable bed.

Pannier
A container such as a basket or leather bag, often in pairs, strapped onto a mule or donkey for carrying loads.

Parquet
Flooring or furniture made of short strips of wood arranged in a geometric pattern.

Parry
Ward off a weapon or attack, often via using a counter move.

Pate
The head, often bald.

Peregrine Falcon
A much-prized falcon because of its fast and accurate flight.

Pewter
A dull-grey metal alloy, made mostly of tin, used for tableware in the Middle Ages.

Plait
A length of braided hair.

Pony
A horse of any small breed.

Portcullis
A strong, heavy grate, used to open or block an opening in a fortress or castle.

Quill Pen
A pen made from a large feather with a hollow stem.

Raven
A large, glossy, blue-black crow, with a hoarse cry, known for its craftiness.

Sconce
In medieval times, a bracket to support a candle or torch attached to a wall.

Scullery
A small kitchen.

Sentry
A soldier stationed to keep guard; a lookout.

Sire or Sir, referring to a knight
Used to address a man of title, a nobleman, or a knight.

Skivvy
A female servant, usually one who performs menial work.

Snee
A small, short dagger.

Soapwort
A plant with leaves that was used to make a soapy substance.

Subtlety course, the
A dish served for entertainment purposes in the Middle Ages (also known as an entremet), often with extravagant decorations, and even live animals. The popular nursery rhyme "Sing a Song of Sixpence" refers to a subtlety when it mentions twenty-four blackbirds baked in a pie.

Sweetmeat
Sweet baked items, such as cake, and/or candied nuts or fruits.

Taper
A slender candle.

Tournament
An event where knights competed in assorted sports and jousts for prizes.

Trencher
A wooden or earthenware platter for serving food.

Whinny
A gentle, high pitched horse's neigh.

Wicca
The practice of witchcraft; a witch.

Wimple
A headdress covering the head, neck, and sides of the face.

Wineskin
An animal skin, sewn together, used to hold wine.

Bibliography

Duggan, Alfred. Growing up in 13th Century England. Toronto: Random House of Canada Ltd., 1962.

Kenyon, Sherrilyn. The Writer's Guide to Everyday Life in the Middle Ages. Cincinnati: F&W Publications Inc., 1995.

Osmond, Edward. The Artist in Britain. London: Studio Books, 1961.

Rowling, Marjorie. Everyday Life in Medieval Times. New York: G.P. Putnam's Sons, 1968.

Tuchman, Barbara. A Distant Mirror: The Calamitous 14th Century. Toronto: Random House of Canada Ltd., 1978. Date of publication.

Author Biography

 Marian Keen, B.S. in Education, Central Connecticut State University, has been writing in a variety of genres since the early 80s. *Verity* intertwines Marian's strong interest in historical fiction, and her deep concern at the growing trend of bullying. Not unique to present day society, the abuse of young people spans the centuries, and, as Verity discovers, the values of integrity, loyalty, and supportive communities can make all the difference.

More information about Marian's other books

Marian Keen has been writing in a variety of genres since the 1980s, with a special interest in historical fiction for children and youth. *Verity* is her first published novel for teens.

Marian's middle-grade stories for children include the adventures of *Alexander Catt*, and the *Lexi Catt* Series. These "meowmoirs" bring to life famous people and significant milestones in science, medicine, art, exploration, and human development. Look out for new titles to be released soon.

Her stories for young readers feature British Columbian animals such as skunks, racoons, owls, bears, squirrels, crows, and seagulls. A complete list of works can be found at megsbooks.com. With a life-long interest in nutrition, healthy living, and illness prevention, Marian's health articles can be found at: stresstonics.com.

Marian's works may be found at megsbooks.com and stresstonics.com.

If you want to get on the path to be a published author with **Influence Publishing** please go to **www.InfluencePublishing.com/InspireABook**

Inspiring books that influence change

More information on our other titles and how to submit your own proposal can be found at **www.InfluencePublishing.com**

CPSIA information can be obtained at www.ICGtesting.com
Printed in the USA
LVOW08s0505080114

368477LV00002B/22/P